122

WE ARE WOLVES

ALSO BY KATRINA NANNESTAD

Rabbit, Soldier, Angel, Thief
The Travelling Bookshop
Olive of Groves and the Great Slurp of Time
Olive of Groves and the Right Royal Romp

RED DIRT DIARIES SERIES

LOTTIE PERKINS SERIES

WE
ARE
WOLVES

Katrina Nannestad

WITH ART BY MARTINA HEIDUCZEK

A CAITLYN DLOUHY BOOK

Atheneum Books for Young Readers
New York London Toronto Sydney New Delhi

A
atheneum ATHENEUM BOOKS FOR YOUNG READERS
An imprint of Simon & Schuster Children's Publishing Division
1230 Avenue of the Americas, New York, New York 10020
This book is a work of fiction. Any references to historical events, real people, or real places are used fictitiously. Other names, characters, places, and events are products of the author's imagination, and any resemblance to actual events or places or persons, living or dead, is entirely coincidental.

For information about special discounts for bulk purchases, please contact Simon & Schuster Special Sales at 1-866-506-1949 or business@simonandschuster.com.
The Simon & Schuster Speakers Bureau can bring authors to your live event. For more information or to book an event, contact the Simon & Schuster Speakers Bureau at 1-866-248-3049 or visit our website at www.simonspeakers.com.
Interior design by Irene Metaxatos
The text for this book was set in Fournier MT Std.
The illustrations for this book were rendered in pencil.
Manufactured in the United States of America
0122 FFG
First Edition
10 9 8 7 6 5 4 3 2 1
Library of Congress Cataloging-in-Publication Data
Names: Nannestad, Katrina, author. | Heiduczek, Martina, illustrator.
Title: We are wolves / Katrina Nannestad ; with illustrations by Martina Heiduczek.
Description: First edition. | New York : Atheneum Books for Young Readers, [2022] | "A Caitlyn Dlouhy book." | Audience: Ages 10 to 14. | Summary: When the Russian army marches into East Prussia at the end of World War II, the Wolf family flees, but Liesl, Otto, and their baby sister, Mia, are separated from their mother, and they are forced to do dangerous things in order to survive.
Identifiers: LCCN 2021023240 | ISBN 9781665904223 (hardcover) | ISBN 9781665904247 (ebook)
Subjects: CYAC: Brothers and sisters—Fiction. | Lost children—Fiction. | Survival—Fiction. | Refugees—Fiction. | World War, 1939-1945—Fiction. | Germans—Lithuania—Fiction. | Prussia, East (Poland and Russia)—Fiction. | Lithuania—Fiction. | LCGFT: Novels. | Historical fiction.
Classification: LCC PZ7.1.N36 We 2022 | DDC [Fic]—dc23
LC record available at https://lccn.loc.gov/2021023240

For my precious sons,
Finn and Klaus

—K. N.

This is a made-up story. The characters are not real, but the wolf children, the *Wolfskinder*, were real.

The wolf children were German children left alone in East Prussia at the end of the Second World War. Lost or orphaned, thousands of these children survived by living wild in the forests and scavenging what food they could from farms, houses, and the land. Many headed north to Lithuania, where life was also hard but food was more abundant. Some were secretly adopted by Lithuanian families, but they had to give up all traces of their German identity. Others worked like slaves in return for food and shelter.

The wolf children were victims of war.

PROUD WOLVES

CHAPTER 1

'Hitler is a toad!'

Our entire household has gathered in the parlor for this big moment—Mama, Papa, Oma, Opa, Otto, Mia, and me—and Otto has decided to go wild.

'Hitler is a toad!' he yells again.

Mama rushes forward and clamps her hand over Otto's mouth, but Otto pushes it away and shouts even louder. 'Hitler is a toad! A big fat toad with warts all over!'

Now Mama clamps her hand to her own mouth.

Papa stands in the middle of us all, dressed in his uniform. He is still Papa but now he is also Soldier Erich Wolf. He has been called up to serve in the German Army and it is more than Otto can bear.

It is more than any of us can bear. But Otto is only seven and he doesn't understand that we must make sacrifices.

For Germany. For our beloved leader, Adolf Hitler. And he doesn't know how to hold the anger, the sadness, and the fear inside.

'Hitler is a toad!' he shouts once more.

Papa drops his rucksack. 'Otto!' he snaps. 'You must not curse Hitler. Ever!'

'It's dangerous!' hisses Mama.

'Terribly dangerous,' whispers Oma.

'And wrong,' I add. 'We love Hitler.'

Papa frowns.

Mama's hand slips from her mouth to her chest.

Opa snorts. Opa seems to be snorting more and more these days. Perhaps he has a cold that just won't go away.

Mia has been silent and staring, but now she pipes up. 'Boo! Boo!' She's only one and a half and it's her favorite thing to say. She's trying to say 'Boom! Boom!' which is Otto's favorite thing to say.

Otto is always playing war games and blowing things up. All the boys are. Otto loves war and battles and tanks and planes and soldiers. But not at this moment. Not when it's our own papa who is becoming a soldier and being sent away from home.

Otto puts his hands on his hips and glares at us all. 'If Hitler is so great, why is his photo turned toward the wall?'

I look over to where Adolf Hitler hangs above the dining table. Otto is right! Our beloved leader is facing the wallpaper. He should be looking into our parlor, shining his goodness and love upon us all, just as he does in every other family's parlor. But he's not. He's facing the wall. Who would do such a thing?

Otto and I both look to Papa. Papa looks to Opa.

Opa shrugs his bony old shoulders and confesses, 'I turned Hitler's portrait to the wall.'

'But why?' I ask.

'Because—' Opa begins.

Mama and Oma glare at him.

'Because . . .' Opa scratches the back of his neck. 'Because you children have the worst table manners in all of East Prussia!'

Otto screws up his nose.

'Otto,' cries Opa, 'you chew with your mouth open so wide, I can see the food all the way down into your stomach. It is a dreadful sight! I do not want our dear, beloved leader, Adolf Hitler, to see that. It is bad enough that your mama and your oma have to watch it!'

'It's true,' says Oma. 'Your papa was the same when he was a little boy.'

Otto blushes, but the corner of his mouth twitches.

'And Mia,' sighs Opa. 'Oh my! I have never seen a baby rub so much porridge and mashed potato into her hair! Adolf Hitler should not have to watch a beautiful little girl turn herself into something that looks like a pile of pig slops!'

Mia looks up at the mention of her name. 'Mia!'

'And Liesl,' Opa growls, rolling his eyes and slapping his

forehead. 'When you cut up your food, your elbows stick out and flap so much that you look like a chicken. I am fearful that you will take flight. An eleven-year-old girl behaving like a silly chicken! Should our dear Führer be exposed to such a ridiculous sight?'

Otto and I are now giggling.

Mama nods at Opa. Opa walks over to the picture and turns it the right way around. Adolf Hitler is looking down on us once more.

'Now, children,' says Papa, his face stern, 'best behavior while I'm gone. Use your manners. Wash behind your ears. And no more rude words about Hitler.'

Opa snorts once more.

'Papa,' coos Mia.

Papa's scowl melts. He drops to his knees and opens his arms wide.

Otto and I rush at him. Mia toddles in. Even Mama joins us. Papa folds himself around us until we are a Papa-Liesl-Otto-Mia-Mama blob. It's our favorite thing to be, this blob.

I press my nose into Papa's coat and breathe deeply. I love the smell of Papa. He is soap and schnapps and nutmeg. But now, in this moment, there is something new, something bitter, like pickled onions. Papa smells of sorrow.

'We'll be fine, Papa,' I mumble into his chest. 'We will be on our best behavior.'

'Yes, Papa,' Otto whispers. 'I won't curse Hitler, and I will chew with my mouth closed from now on.'

Mia giggles—a bubbly baby giggle that makes me want to join in.

But Papa still smells like pickled onions.

'Please, Papa,' I beg, 'don't be sad. The war will end soon and you'll come home and we'll have an enormous party.'

'Yes. Yes!' agrees Papa.

The blob falls apart. Papa kisses Mama on each eyelid. He pecks Oma on the forehead. And last of all, he shakes his father's hand.

Opa must feel like that isn't enough because he reels Papa in by his arm until they are hugging, pressing their cheeks together, their tears mingling.

And then Papa is gone.

Otto and I run to the window and slip behind the curtains. We lean on the windowsill and watch as Papa walks away down the street. His newly cut hair bristles at the back of his soldier's cap. His right foot drags behind him, catching on the cobblestones. It's because of his bad leg, the one that was squashed beneath a horse when he was just a boy. The one that has stopped him from being a soldier. Until now: October 1944. So many years into the war.

Otto leans against me like he always does when he's sad. I wrap my arm around him and squeeze him into my side.

We watch as Papa stops in the middle of the street. He is joined by the others from our village who have been called up, at last, to serve as soldiers in the glorious German Army. There is Herr Wagner, who has three fingers missing, Herr

Schmidt, who has a glass eye, and Jakob, from three doors down. Jakob's uniform is too big. It has been made for a man, but Jakob is a skinny sixteen-year-old boy. He looks like a scarecrow with his sleeves flapping down over his fingertips.

'Four new soldiers,' I say.

'No, five!' shouts Otto. 'Look! Hitler even wants Herr Beck in his army.' Otto turns to me, his blue eyes wide. 'Herr Beck is ancient, Liesl—almost as old as Opa. And he's deaf! As deaf as a post!'

Otto is right. Herr Beck is a clockmaker, and I expect all that ticking and chiming has worn out his eardrums. The other day I called hello as I passed his shop, and he replied, 'Yes, yes, business is slow these days.'

We watch as Herr Beck huffs and puffs to catch up to Papa. Papa holds the old man's arm while he gets his breath back. Then, together, Hitler's new soldiers disappear down the street—three old men, a boy, and a limping papa. They will all be heroes soon, when Germany wins the war.

'Hans and Wolfgang are playing in the street!' shouts Otto. He flaps through the curtains back into the sitting room. 'Mama! Mama! Can I go out to play?' Otto leaps from sadness to joy so easily.

Mama blinks as though she can't quite remember where she is. 'Of course,' she says, her voice flat. 'Take Mia with you. Her stroller is by the door. A bit of fresh air will do you both good.'

Otto swoops Mia up from the floor and runs into the hallway. Mia squeals with delight and fear as he tosses her into the stroller and rattles her down the steps into the street. I stay at the window and watch as he runs toward Hans and Wolfgang, pushing Mia in her stroller, making tank noises.

'Chug! Chug! Chug!' he shouts. 'Boom! Boom! Boom!'

Mia jiggles and yells, 'Boo! Boo! Boo!'

I slip out from behind the curtains. Mama and Oma have disappeared into the kitchen to make our supper. Opa has returned to the basement to mend our boots. I am all alone.

I look at the Papa-shaped sag in his armchair. I flop into it, close my eyes, and breathe in. Soap. Schnapps. Nutmeg.

'Soon,' I whisper. 'Papa will be home again soon.'

CHAPTER 2

'Opa,' I call from the top of the basement stairs. 'Supper is ready.'

'Come down here, Liesl,' Opa calls back. 'I have a surprise for you.'

I creep down the steps, careful not to fall. It's so dark, I don't know how Opa can see a thing. But as I near the workbench, he turns up the oil lamp.

'Ta-da!' Opa spreads his hands toward his creation. 'Brand-new boots for my Liesl!'

I gasp and step back. Opa has taken two pairs of boots that are so old and worn they are no longer any use and made them into one new pair. It's a clever idea except that one boot is brown while the other is black. The toes and lace holes are a little different too.

'They're . . . They're . . . ,' I stutter.

'Just like the boots in the fairy tale about the elves and the shoemaker,' says Opa. 'The finest in the land!'

That's *not* what I was thinking. 'They're . . .' I bite my lip.

'Unique!' cries Opa. 'And they have no holes and will keep your feet warm and dry when the snow comes!'

I blush. Of course, he is right. I should be grateful. Warm, watertight boots are a treat and more than many folk have nowadays. All of the new boots in East Prussia — and the rest of Germany—go to our soldiers. Which is proper because they are fighting to make Germany great. And when the war is over, we will all have shiny new boots whenever we like, I am sure.

'Thank you, Opa,' I say. 'They're lovely.'

'And unique, don't forget,' says Opa, his eyes twinkling.

I laugh. 'Yes, they are!'

Oma has set the table with our best china and fine linen napkins. We have soup made with potatoes and carrots. I hate carrots. But then we have cake. A real cake with cherries in the middle and cream on top. Mama walked from farm to farm until she managed to buy enough eggs, butter, and cream to bake something truly special.

'To cheer us all up,' she says.

And for a while it does. Mia grins with the first mouthful of buttery sweetness and soon she has cream rubbed into her hair alongside the pieces of squashed potato.

Opa pretends to be horrified. 'Disgusting! Disgusting!' he roars, throwing his hands in the air.

But his silly faces and mock cries of despair encourage Mia. She grins and gurgles and rubs a half-chewed cherry into her golden curls.

'When it's my birthday,' says Otto, 'I want a cake just like this . . . except chocolate . . . with nuts on top . . . and no cherries in the middle . . . and icing instead of cream.'

'So a different cake altogether,' says Mama.

'Exactly!' cries Otto, and we all burst out laughing.

'I remember the first cake I ever made for Opa,' says Oma. 'It was three days after our wedding, and I decided it would be romantic to bake something delicious for my new husband.'

'Was it good, Opa?' I ask. 'Did you think it was romantic? Did you kiss Oma to say thank you?'

'No,' says Opa. 'I took one bite and spat it into the sink.'

Oma laughs. 'I used salt instead of sugar, by mistake. Apparently, that matters quite a lot for the success of a cake.'

'And for the success of a marriage!' adds Opa.

Oma reaches across the table and grabs Opa's hand. 'Ah, but we've had a long and happy marriage despite my dreadful cooking, haven't we, Friedrich?'

'Yes, yes, we have,' Opa says, and sighs.

I swallow my last mouthful of cake, but it catches in my throat. Something about Opa's words hurts. He makes it sound as though the long years of happiness have ended.

At bedtime, Mama lays Mia in her cot and we sing her favorite nursery rhyme, 'All My Ducklings.' Mia babbles along and makes her hands into beaks for the ducklings, doves, chickens, and goslings. Then we sing her lullabies filled with stars and angels, roses and sheep, until she falls asleep.

Mama tucks Otto and me into our big bed and tells us a story. 'Once upon a time there was a king who had twelve daughters—'

'No! No!' shouts Otto. 'There was a soldier. A German soldier. And his name was Otto.'

The war has taken over our bedtime stories just as it has Otto's games. He was only two when the war started—too young to remember any other life.

Mama nods and tries again. 'Once upon a time there was a soldier called Otto and a beautiful, downtrodden girl called Cinderella—'

'No! No! No!' shouts Otto. 'The girl is called Liesl.'

It's the same every night. Mama tells the story and Otto interrupts all the way through. Otto is always the brave German soldier who wins battles against bears, vicious ravens, enchanted fish, wicked witches, the British Air Force, the American Navy, and the Russian Army. Sometimes there is just one enemy, but usually there will be a combination— ferocious bears working alongside the Russian Army, eye-pecking ravens flying through the sky with the British Air Force, hungry fish waiting for the American Navy to sink a ship so they can eat all the sailors as they flounder in the water.

Every night, a helpless girl called Liesl is among those

in distress, and she is always crying and thanking Otto the soldier for saving her life. It's annoying, but at least every story ends with Liesl and Otto going home to a cottage where there is a blazing fire and an enormous dinner, and they live happily ever after. All stories need a happily-ever-after.

Mama finishes tonight's story with roast pork and mashed potatoes—she's careful to avoid carrots for my sake—and tucks the eiderdown duvet beneath our chins. Mia snores softly. How she can sleep through Mama's stories with Otto's shouting and sound effects is a mystery.

'Papa loves Mia's soft baby snores,' I whisper.

Mama sits back down on our bed. 'Yes. And he loves the way Otto sleeps with his toy airplane stuffed beneath the pillow. And he loves the way you are kind to everyone, Liesl. Papa loves everything about you all.'

'Mama,' I say. 'Is it true that the war is almost over?'

She tucks a stray wisp of my hair behind my ear before answering. 'Yes, Liesl, the war will soon be done.'

I smile, but Mama does not. She leans forward and kisses my forehead, keeping her lips against my skin for a long time. When she pulls away, her eyes are shiny.

Mama leaves the room, but sorrow lingers in the air, and I am confused.

CHAPTER 3

The cold autumn wind whips my cheeks and freezes my fingers. I've lost one of my red mittens. My right hand is warm and snuggly, but my left hand is miserable. I think it's turning blue.

School will be cold too, because there is no coal for the fires. There's wood, but not enough, and my teacher, Fräulein Hofmann, won't light the fire until winter arrives.

I look down at my strange new boots—one brown, one black. At least my feet are warm, thanks to Opa.

Otto runs circles around me, arms stretched wide. He's pretending to be a plane and is dropping imaginary bombs along the street. 'Boom! Boom! Boom!'

Just as we round the corner and arrive at school, I begin to sneeze. I sneeze over and over again. Fräulein Hofmann is standing at the front steps and asks if I am ill.

'I'm fine, thank you,' I say. 'It's the dust and ash from Königsberg. There's so much of it in the air when the wind comes from the west.'

'Liesl Wolf, that's ridiculous!' snaps Fräulein Hofmann. 'The city of Königsberg is far, far away. Besides, it's two months since it was bombed, and those silly British pilots missed their targets completely. All they hit were a few derelict warehouses on the edge of the city.'

Otto zooms in and lands between me and my teacher. 'We watched from Mama and Papa's bedroom window!' he shouts. 'We could feel the explosions and see the glow from the fires. And then the British pilots came back three nights later and bombed it all over again.'

'Just warehouses!' snaps Fräulein Hofmann. 'The British did us a favor, getting rid of all those rat-infested old shacks.'

'Rats!' cries Otto. He flies off across the schoolyard, arms stretched wide. Now he is bombing all the rats in East Prussia. 'Boom! Boom! Boom!'

I smile at Fräulein Hofmann. I am glad to know that nothing important was bombed in Königsberg and even happier that nobody was hurt. Except for the rats.

I sneeze again. 'Perhaps it's a cold after all,' I say.

Fräulein Hofmann nods and smiles. 'Of course it's a cold. Königsberg is fine, Liesl. East Prussia is fine. Germany is strong.' She puffs out her chest. 'We are *not* losing the war.'

I stare at her. Who said anything about Germany losing the war?

Our schoolroom is crowded with sixty-three students: two classes squashed together because the male teachers are off fighting in the war, and Otto's teacher, Fräulein Rothschild, just disappeared. Teachers are in short supply, like boots and meat and papas.

Fräulein Hofmann doesn't seem to mind. She's having a wonderful time, running our lessons like a military operation. She shouts like a sergeant major commanding his soldiers.

'Stand!'

'Sing "The Song of the Germans"!'

'Sit!'

'Take out your books!'

'Write your nine times table!'

'Liesl, tell us the answer to eighty times seventy.'

I love school. I love learning. I love the way Fräulein Hofmann keeps everything running on a tight schedule. And I especially love the lessons about Germany and how we are bringing civilization and joy to more and more countries across the globe. I even love the crowded classroom. More bodies means more heat.

On the way home, Otto is flying about, bombing rats in Königsberg once more, when suddenly he stops.

'Liesl!' he cries, grabbing my hand so that I, too, must come to a halt. 'Can you hear that?'

Above the howling wind, I hear boots. Heavy boots, marching along the cobblestones.

Otto drags me back the way we have come, until we are

standing in front of the school watching hundreds and hundreds of soldiers march by. They are young and handsome and hold their heads high.

'Hooray! Hooray!' cries Otto. 'Good luck! Good luck against those rotten Russians and the rats!'

One of the soldiers turns his head and winks. 'We don't need luck!' he shouts. 'We have might and right and Adolf Hitler on our side!'

We smile, wave, and cheer at the soldiers as they pass. Some ignore us, but others salute and hand us treats—three chocolate bars and a can of condensed milk. Treasure!

'Heil Hitler!' I shout as the soldiers disappear down the street.

As one, they raise their right arms in the air and reply, 'Heil Hitler!'

My heart swells with pride and I can feel goose bumps on my arms. This is an exciting time to be German!

We eat the chocolate bars on the way home, silently, letting every square melt slowly on our tongues. We should be sharing them with Mia, Mama, Oma, and Opa, but we can't help ourselves. It's so very long since we had real chocolate.

Otto's grin is wide and gooey at the corners. 'I love the war!' he cries. 'Except for Papa being gone.'

'If you think *this* is good,' I say, handing him the last of the chocolate, 'just wait until the war is over!'

CHAPTER 4

It is the twenty-third of December, and Mama and I are Christmas shopping. Not for presents, but for food. It's a special outing, just the two of us.

Normally, I'd be at school on a Saturday, but not now when the winter has grown so harsh. We go to school for shorter hours and not at all on Saturday, which saves on firewood. By the time we arrive on Monday, the classroom is so cold after sitting empty for the weekend that there is ice on the windowpanes—inside as well as out—and our fingers and toes feel like stone.

Yesterday, Otto tried to lick the ice from the window, and his tongue got stuck. Fräulein Hofmann had to breathe on the glass until the ice softened enough for Otto and his silly tongue to pull free. I thought she would be furious, that she would shout like a commandant. But when Otto was free, she gave him a hug and spoke to him softly, gently.

'Think before you act, my boy. It is important, Otto . . . now more than ever. Be sensible. Stay safe. Please, Otto.'

They were kind words, and I was glad that Otto wasn't scolded, but I felt strange afterward. A little squirmy in the stomach. Scared without knowing why.

But that was yesterday. Today I am happy, holding Mama's hand as we walk along the lanes, leaping over frozen puddles, singing Christmas songs, and laughing. It has been so long since I have heard Mama laugh.

We are going from farm to farm at the edge of our village, buying anything fresh that might help make a feast for tomorrow night. We are lucky that we live in the country where there are animals and rich fields for growing vegetables and grain. East Prussia is called the breadbasket of Germany. Maybe it should be called the milk can and the soup pot, too! But whatever we call it, we are lucky. Especially so because Mama knows the secret to gathering a fine meal.

'Never ask for too much, Liesl,' she explains. 'Just one egg here, a small onion there, a worm-eaten cabbage at the next place. And always pay well. We can't eat money, but a hearty meal will keep us fat and merry for a few more days.' Mama pats her skinny stomach, and we both laugh.

After two hours, our milk can sloshes with cream and our basket is full—four potatoes, an enormous turnip, four eggs, a tiny cabbage (with wormholes, just as Mama expected), and half a sausage. A real pork sausage that smells of meat and spice.

'We'll have a splendid Christmas Eve!' I cry. 'All we need now is for Papa to come home and join us.'

Mama stops. 'Liesl, Papa is a soldier now. You know that. He can't come home anytime he likes.'

'But it's Christmas, Mama, and the soldiers are sometimes given leave to be with their families. Ruth's papa was home last Christmas for a whole week.' I smile at her. 'So why not our papa? Wouldn't it be wonderful!'

I dance around Mama and slip on the ice. Mama helps me to my feet.

'Yes,' she agrees, 'it would be wonderful. Just . . . Just don't get your hopes up, Liesl.'

The air that was so full of joy and hope moments ago becomes cold and heavy.

But Mama's smile returns, and she says, 'There's one more thing to do before we go home.'

She strides ahead, and I must run to catch up. We walk briskly and silently until we arrive at the Kruger farm. Frau Kruger meets us at the gate, a dead goose in her hand, hanging upside down by the legs. Its eyes are closed, and it looks perfect, like it is simply sleeping.

'Greetings and Merry Christmas for tomorrow,' Mama says kindly.

Frau Kruger nods but says nothing. She stares at Mama, her eyes wide, her mouth open.

Mama reaches into her pocket and pulls out a white

handkerchief tied into a bundle. She picks open the knot. Inside sits her beautiful pearl necklace, and I wonder why she has brought it to this farm.

But then Frau Kruger snatches the pearls with her plump fingers and passes the goose to me. Mama has bought this goose with her precious pearls. She has paid too much!

The dead goose swings back and forth from my hand, and I wait for Mama to object.

Instead, she says, 'Thank you, Frau Kruger.'

The farmer's wife doesn't reply. She is staring greedily at the pearls.

Silly woman, I think. *Mama's beautiful pearls will look ridiculous with your milking smock and muddy clogs!*

A bitter feeling wells up inside me, but it's quickly pushed aside by tummy rumblings and mouth waterings as I imagine the roast goose that will crowd our Christmas table tomorrow night.

We make our way back through the village toward home. The wind is icy, but we are warm from the effort of carrying our goodies and the thoughts of the delicious feast ahead.

'Onions and bread crumbs and almonds,' sighs Mama, her eyes almost closed as she describes the stuffing she'll make for the goose.

'What about currants?' I ask hopefully. 'Or raisins?'

'Yes, yes! Both!' says Mama. 'If I can find any. And nutmeg. Lots and lots of nutmeg! It will be the best stuffing I have ever made.'

'The best stuffing I have ever *tasted*!' I clutch the heavy goose to my chest.

We turn the corner and see a column of soldiers marching along our street.

No. Not marching. They are straggling. Some are carried on stretchers.

Mama cries out. She drops her basket to the ground, and her hand flies to her mouth.

We creep forward. We stand so close to the passing soldiers that we can smell sour sweat, burned metal, fear. Heads, hands, and knees are wrapped in bandages. Not clean white bandages like we use in first-aid practice at school, but muddy, stained rags. Eyes are dull.

'Poor boys,' Mama murmurs. 'What have we done to you?'

We? I think. *No. What have they done to you?*

A man being carried on a stretcher reaches out and grabs Mama's skirt. His hand is filthy, and there's blood beneath his fingernails. I want to tell him to let my mama go. But Mama steps forward and places her hand gently on his cheek.

'Frau,' he whispers, 'it is bad. Far worse than they are telling you.' He's carried on before he can say more.

'What does he mean?' I ask. But Mama says nothing.

We stand in silence and stare as the soldiers limp by. One or two nod in our direction, but most keep their eyes forward or down to their boots. They are so very different from the brave young men who gave Otto and me the chocolate.

I wish there was something I could do. Something to cheer them up. Something to remind them that the war is almost over and soon there will be nothing but happiness and roast goose and fancy parades.

Then, suddenly, I know what I can do. I pass the goose to Mama, run after the soldiers, thrust my hand in the air, and shout, 'Heil Hitler!'

But nobody lifts a hand. Nobody says a word.

CHAPTER 5

Opa, Otto, and I are in the bathroom. I'm cleaning my teeth. Otto is cleaning Opa's teeth.

Otto loves Opa's false teeth. He holds them in his hand and brushes them softly, as though he is grooming a mouse or a baby squirrel.

'Opa,' says Otto, 'when I have finished cleaning your teeth, can I play with them?'

Opa chuckles. 'No, no! Then it will be time to clean your own teeth.' His words are fuzzy at the edges, because it's hard to speak properly through bare gums.

'Pleeeease.' Otto blinks up at Opa, his blue eyes as big and round as Mama's cake plates.

'Absolutely not!' cries Opa. 'I know what you will do. You will drive them around the parlor floor making tank noises, and then I'll always be thinking of my teeth as a weapon of war. When the Russians come, I'll feel obliged to surrender my teeth!'

Otto giggles, but I feel sick. Why would the Russians be coming onto German soil?

I think of the soldiers we saw this afternoon. And then I think of that one soldier's words: 'It is bad. Far worse than they are telling you.' I shiver.

When our teeth are done, Opa tucks Otto into bed while I go downstairs to tell Mama we are ready for our story.

Mama and Oma are whispering in the kitchen. I know I shouldn't eavesdrop, but I'm sure they are talking about our Christmas presents, and I'm bursting to know what it is that Oma and Mama have been making for me these last four weeks. Christmas Eve is just a sleep away, but it seems like an eternity to wait. I step up to the crack in the door and hold my breath.

'Pearls!' hisses Oma. 'Pearls for a goose, Anna. How could you?'

'It was the only way,' says Mama. 'Frau Kruger wouldn't give us a goose for anything less.'

'Give?' Oma draws in a sharp breath. 'It was not *given*. It came at a great price.'

Mama sighs. 'Yes. But it might be the last Christmas the children will get to celebrate for a long time. When the war is over—'

'When the war is over, we will need all our pearls and jewels and silver and gold to survive,' Oma snaps. 'A mere scrap of bread will cost a diamond. You were Otto's age when the last war ended; you must remember what it was like afterward—the hunger, the cold, the disease. A goose might be fun for the children for a day or two, but at what price?'

There is a long silence, and cold air seems to leak from the kitchen, through the crack in the door and into my body. I shiver once more.

I don't go into the kitchen to ask for a story. Instead I creep back upstairs, crawl into bed beside Otto, and wait.

When Mama comes up at last, we sing Mia a nursery rhyme about baking a cake. The baker needs eggs and lard, butter and salt, milk and flour and saffron. As we sing our way through the ingredients, my voice falters, then Mama's does too, and Otto has to finish the song alone.

After Mia falls asleep, Mama starts our bedtime story, but tonight it is flat and boring. Mama's heart isn't in it. Otto tries to give her all the right words, but in the end Mama gives up.

'I'm sorry, children,' she sighs. 'I'm tired, and there's still so much to be done for our Christmas celebrations.'

She kisses our foreheads, then leaves.

Otto is not satisfied. 'I can't sleep without a proper bedtime story. Liesl, tell me a story about what it will be like at the end of the war.'

I remember Oma's words about people being so hungry they would pay a diamond for one scrap of bread. I feel sick at the thought of how much it would cost to bake the cake in Mia's nursery rhyme.

'I can't, Otto,' I whisper. 'I'm too sleepy.'

What I really mean is that I'm too scared. Too confused.

But Otto will not settle. He grumbles and grunts and wriggles and kicks until I decide that it's easier to give in. I close my eyes and dig down through the scary new images that have been planted in my mind until I get to the shiny golden pictures that Adolf Hitler and Fräulein Hofmann have been painting for me since I first started school.

'When the war is over,' I begin, 'Germany will stretch across the entire world, and the sun will shine down on us. There will be celebrations in every town, even little villages like ours. There will be a parade right past our house, the soldiers marching and singing and throwing hundreds and hundreds of chocolate bars into the crowd—at least three for every person. Even for babies like Mia. Everyone will be wearing new clothes and their boots will match, and the ladies will have stockings and red lipstick. Adolf Hitler will do a grand tour of Germany, and, if we are lucky, he will come to our school and we'll perform "The Song of the Germans" for him. I will wear a blue dress with . . .'

Otto has fallen asleep, his toy plane hugged to his chest, a smile on his face. But I carry on with the story, our life after the war growing more and more fantastic.

'I will wear a blue dress with a white lace collar and a wide satin ribbon around the waist, and Adolf Hitler will say, "My, Liesl Wolf, what a fine German girl you are!" The fountains will flow with lemonade, and not just on the day the

Führer visits, but every single day until winter comes again. Then the fountains will be full of ice cream. Chocolate ice cream and strawberry ice cream. And we will get a puppy for Christmas—one each year, so that soon our house will be full of sausage dogs, yipping and yapping and chewing the laces from our shiny new boots. Every Saturday we will go all the way to the beach for a school picnic, where we will eat nothing but gingerbread and marzipan, and the sun will shine again, and the water in Vistula Lagoon will be as warm as a bath.'

I go on and on and on until I start to believe my own words, because it is easier than believing the horrible things I have heard today—in the streets and in my own home.

I take a deep breath and finish my story with the best part of all: 'And Papa will come home and gather us into a Papa-Liesl-Otto-Mia-Mama blob, and we will live happily ever after.'

CHAPTER 6

We are gathered around the table. It's Christmas Eve, and nothing matters except this moment.

Otto grins at me, goose fat making his lips and chin shiny. He chews with his mouth open and flies his toy airplane across the gravy jug.

Mia rubs a giant goose drumstick back and forth across her head, and everyone claps and cheers as though it is the cleverest thing a baby has ever done.

Mia drops the drumstick and claps too, her chubby baby hands slipping and sliding across each other, and shouts, 'Goose!'

'Clever girl!' coos Mama. 'You've learned a new word. Goose! Goose!'

'Goose! Goose!' repeats Mia. She picks up her drumstick again and flings it across the table at Otto. 'Boo! Boo!'

Otto points the drumstick at Mia like a cannon and shouts, 'Boom! Boom!'

'No, children,' says Oma. 'No war games today. Christmas is a time of peace and joy.'

Oma is right. Here, now, our parlor is filled with both.

The food in our tummies is making us happy and relaxed. And in the corner, by Papa's chair, is a tree. It's tiny, barely as tall as the armchair, and there are only five candles flickering on the branches and three presents underneath—one each for Mia, Otto, and me. But it is beautiful.

Oma keeps piling our plates with mashed potato and cabbage, and when we are all stuffed full, she clears everything away and brings out marzipan for dessert. Real marzipan!

Just when I think things couldn't possibly get any better, there is a knock at the door. A loud, clear knock. It is Papa! I just know it. Adolf Hitler's Christmas gift to the Wolf family is sending our papa home on leave for Christmas. But I don't say so, because it will spoil the surprise.

Mama is trying to show Mia how to put marzipan into her mouth rather than into her ear, so I jump to my feet and shout, 'I'll get it!'

I make myself walk into the hallway, not run. I want to savor this moment, the tightly held excitement that will soon explode into fireworks of joy. I imagine Papa's face splitting wide with a smile that will light up the room more than a million candles. I can see Mama's happy tears and hear Oma singing out, 'A Christmas miracle!' Opa will be speechless for once, but his eyes will shine when he sees his son.

I stop, wipe my mouth on the back of my hand, and straighten my dress. Then I open the front door . . . and stare.

It's a boy, just a little older than me. He is wearing a uniform and has a satchel slung over his shoulder. His bike rests on the wall between our house and the one next door.

I have never seen him before, but instantly I hate him. He is a telegram delivery boy. The telegrams these boys bring do not say lovely things like *Christmas greetings from Aunty Ilsa*, or *Congratulations! You have won a trip to Munich to see a parade*. These telegrams bring news from the war. News about loved ones. And it is always bad.

I step back. If I slam the door, the boy will have to leave, and our Christmas supper will carry on with laughter and clapping and marzipan. We haven't even made it to the presents yet.

But I stumble, and before I can shut the boy out, he leaps up the steps and pokes the telegram into my hand.

'Sorry,' he mutters, and slinks away.

I stare at the envelope, frozen to the spot, until I hear a knock on the neighbor's door. The boy hands a second telegram to Jakob's mother. Jakob, the boy soldier who marched off to war with my papa.

Jakob's mother lets out a howl. She sounds more like a dog than a woman.

Krista, Jakob's younger sister, runs to the doorstep and whimpers at the sight of the telegram in her mother's hand.

And then, across the gap between our homes, her eyes meet mine.

I open and close my mouth. Krista stares at me.

We do not say a word.

'Missing in action.' Mama reads the words aloud as we all stand around her, stupid, useless.

Oma clings to Opa, shaking.

Mama stares at the telegram in her hand.

I hug Mia to my chest and try to breathe. 'No, no, no,' Mia whimpers, and I realize that I'm squeezing her too tightly.

'Missing in action,' Mama reads for the second time.

Papa is missing. It is Christmas Eve and he has been gone just two months, but it's long enough for him to be missing. My red mitten is missing. I have looked for it everywhere, but I can't find it. I think it's lost forever. Is it the same with Papa?

Otto seems to think so, because his blue eyes have turned gray and his cheeks are burning red and, before we can stop him, he explodes.

'Hitler is a rat! Hitler took my papa away and now he won't give him back!'

'Otto! Shoosh!' cries Oma.

She wobbles forward to grab Otto, to cover his mouth, but Otto is fast. He is across the room and has flung open the window, and now he's shouting into the street for everyone to hear.

'Hitler is a rat! A big, fat, dirty rat who lies!'

Opa grabs Otto by the collar of his shirt and pulls him back inside. He slams the window shut, then presses Otto to his chest until my brother quietens.

'Otto!' Mama gasps. 'You mustn't. It's dangerous. So dangerous. People who curse Hitler are taken away, and they never come back.'

I feel sick at Mama's words.

Otto looks up from Opa's chest. His face is a muddle of anger, sorrow, and fear.

'Otto, you made a promise to Papa!' I burst out. 'Remember? You said you would be good. You promised you would never say bad things about Hitler again.'

'Papa isn't here!' Otto is screaming again. 'He's gone, Liesl! Hitler sent Papa away, and he is never *ever* coming back!'

'We don't know that,' I whisper. 'Missing is just lost, like my red mitten.' And then I say what I don't even believe. 'Mittens turn up again when you least expect them to—usually in the summer when you no longer need them. Papa is probably just lost in a forest somewhere.' My voice falters. 'He'll wander out in the springtime and come home for Easter, and we will all laugh about it.'

Otto pulls away from Opa. He stands in the middle of the room, hands squeezed into fists, glaring at us all.

'Missing is dead,' he says. 'It just means they can't find a body.'

I sob. Otto is only seven. He shouldn't know such things. None of us should know such things.

CHAPTER 7

Opa walks around the house muttering. Angry words. Dangerous words. And suddenly I know where Otto got his Hitler curses. He must have heard Opa's grumblings. Once secret. Now slipping out into the open, more and more.

'Just you wait and see!' Opa roars at Oma across the kitchen. 'Now that the cripples like my Erich and the boys like Jakob are gone, they will be sending old men and women like us, and boys as young as Otto into battle! Who knows? They may come knocking for baby Mia before the day is over!'

'Friedrich!' shouts Oma. 'Liesl is here. Don't say such things.'

Mama goes to bed and doesn't get up again for three days. When she comes out, she is pale and thin and her eyes have sunk into her face. She walks straight into the parlor and turns Adolf Hitler's portrait toward the wall.

'Mama,' I whisper.

Mama lifts her hand. 'Enough. Enough with the lies.'

Before I can ask what she means, she is gone. And I hear her bedroom door close once more.

CHAPTER 8

It is the twelfth of January when Opa announces, 'School is canceled.'

He is holding Mia in his arms and she claps her hands together as though this is the best news she has ever heard.

Otto agrees. 'Hooray!' he shouts. 'No school! No lessons! No spelling!'

He grabs his toy airplane and flies it around the kitchen, weaving in and out of the chairs and around Oma as she chops onions and cabbage for the soup.

We haven't been to school since Christmas. The winter has been too harsh. Everything is frozen. At first they said we would go back in the middle of January, but now school is canceled. 'Canceled' sounds like a long time.

I am disappointed. I miss my lessons and the routine and

the stories Fräulein Hofmann tells about Germany and its glorious future.

'When will school start again?' I ask.

Opa shrugs. 'Perhaps when the snow stops falling.'

'Maybe when school starts again,' says Otto, 'we'll have to keep the fire going by burning our chairs and desks, and we'll have to sit on the floor.' His eyes shine. 'Perhaps we'll burn our pencils and rulers, too.'

Oma shakes her head, but Otto's words aren't so silly. Even here at home we are freezing most of the time. Our wood is saved for the kitchen stove where Oma cooks. The fireplace in the parlor remains cold and empty, so the parlor remains cold and empty. Except for Adolf Hitler, who stays in there alone, staring at the wallpaper.

'Come, come!' shouts Opa. 'Pull up a chair. We'll sit by the stove and do some lessons of our own.'

Otto slumps. He looks straight at the soup pot and drones, 'Good morning, Fräulein Hofmann.'

Oma rolls her eyes, but Opa chuckles, and soon we are all laughing. Even Oma.

Otto and I spend the rest of the morning reciting poetry, saying our times tables, and reading stories to Opa, Mia, and Fräulein Hofmann the soup pot. It makes us laugh, on and on and on.

Once, at the very moment Otto says that five times four is fifteen, the soup bubbles over the top of the pot and hisses on the stove. It is just like Fräulein Hofmann, the way she

seethes and froths in anger when Otto has drifted into a day-
dream and given yet another silly answer to one of her questions. We stare wide-eyed at the soup pot, then burst into a
fresh round of laughter.

Everything should feel dull and unimportant since the
telegram about Papa, but somehow it doesn't. We still manage
to make it through each day. Most of the time it's as though
he is still just away and will come home when the war is done.
We work. We play. We eat. We laugh. We forget.

And then, at unexpected moments, we remember.

It is almost lunchtime, and Mia is dozing in Opa's arms.
I start reading the story of Hansel and Gretel to Otto. I have
barely mentioned the woodcutter papa when Mia opens her
eyes and shouts, 'Papa! Papa!'

My breath catches.

'Papa!' says Mia. 'Want Papa!'

Oma drops the baking pan. It clatters to the floor, but no
one picks it up. For Mia has just spoken her first sentence. We
should be proud, delighted. We should be cheering at this clever
thing our little sister has done. But she has used her very first
sentence to ask for something we cannot give. 'Want Papa!'
Mia shouts, and bounces up and down in Opa's lap and claps
her hands. She looks around at each of us, waiting. 'Mia! Papa!'

Otto stands, opens the stove door, snatches the book of
fairy tales from my hands, and throws it into the fire. Our
beautiful, precious book!

Opa barely raises an eyebrow, and I am so cold that, for

a moment, my heart leaps for joy at the huge flames and the warmth the book gives off. But before the pages are fully burned, I am cold once more, and my face is drenched with tears.

I dress warmly and slip out the front door. I need to get out. I need to be alone.

I walk right into the middle of the street and stop. My nose throbs with the cold and I have to breathe into my scarf to stop my lungs from aching, but the world outside is beautiful. Snow is falling thickly and everything is white. The houses look like a picture from a storybook, and it is so beautiful, so peaceful, that it's hard to believe anything bad could happen here.

I take my hands out of my pockets and stare at my mittens. Two mittens. Both red. Brilliant against the white snow. One was missing, but now it is found. It was stuffed down the side of Mia's stroller. I didn't even have to wait until springtime for it to reappear.

A mitten. A papa.

Hope flickers.

I stand in the silent, white street and wonder. The snow falls, heavier and heavier.

I don't know how long I have been there when a cow comes charging down the street toward me. A cow! Outside in the snow! She is large and powerful with long horns.

I know I should be scared. I should go inside. But I don't.

I stay in the middle of the road, frozen to the spot.

The cow runs with her head down, but as she approaches me, she slows to a trot, then stops. I stare at her, and our eyes meet. She steps closer and sniffs around my chest and neck. Then she stretches out her wide pink tongue and licks my cheek. Her tongue is rough and dry but sends tingles through my body.

'Thank you,' I whisper.

The cow blinks and plods silently away.

The tingles surge through me. And hope, too. Strange things happen.

A cow wanders through the snow and licks a girl's cheek.

A lost mitten reappears.

A papa who is missing can be found.

Mama comes out of her bedroom for supper. She smiles and kisses each of us on the head. Mia. Otto. Me.

I tell everyone about the cow and the new hope in my heart.

Otto frowns into his soup. 'Getting excited about a cow is stupid. It would be far better if it was Papa running along the street and licking your cheek.'

'Papa wouldn't lick my cheek,' I retort, because I don't know what else to say. The cow matters, but I can't explain why.

Oma smiles and says, 'Hope is good, Liesl. I'm glad you saw the cow.'

But when Otto and I head for bed and sit on the bottom

step to unlace our boots, we hear Mama, Oma, and Opa talking in the kitchen. Oma isn't so excited about the cow now.

'A cow,' she sighs. 'In this snow. Poor thing.'

'I hear there are cattle wandering all over East Prussia,' Opa grumbles. 'Sometimes whole herds freezing in the snow. They're from the front where the Russians have been. Their barns have been blown to bits, and now they're running scared. And *we* should be running scared too!'

'We can't run,' says Oma. 'Those who flee will be punished. You know that, Friedrich. We have been ordered to stand and defend!'

I look down at my brother, confused. People who are winning a war don't need to defend their land. Besides, who is left to fight against the Russian Army? Old men like Opa, women like Oma and Mama, and children like Otto and Mia and me. What could we do? Wave our rolling pins and walking sticks, our rattles and schoolbooks, at the Red Army's tanks and cannons to scare them away?

But Oma won't see sense. 'We should be preparing to flee,' Opa says. 'We should be packing, sorting out what is necessary and useful for a long, dangerous journey. And then we should run before the Russians get here. Before it's too late.'

There is a loud noise. I jump in fright, and my boot falls to the floor. I think Opa has banged his hand down on the table.

I leave my boot where it landed, grab Otto by the hand, and run upstairs to bed.

Nobody comes to tuck us in.

Otto is awake but silent. I stare at the dark ceiling.

Mia grizzles in her cot. She's probably cold, so I bring her into our bed, squeezing her into the warm nook between Otto and me. We sing her a lullaby, one filled with sheep and lambs and stars. Soon she is snoring.

'Are the Russians really coming?' whispers Otto.

'No,' I say firmly. 'Of course not. The German Army is invincible.'

'But Opa said . . .' Otto's voice fades. He can't bear to say it out loud.

I chew my lip and my head spins as I grasp for something that will comfort my brother. Something that will comfort me.

'I know what Opa said,' I whisper. 'But it's all a trick. The German Army is *pretending* to be weak. The Russians will barge into East Prussia, where they'll be met by the German Army and defeated.' I slap my hands on the eiderdown and grin. 'And the war will be over, and all the lost papas and all the lost cows will find their way home once more.'

'But what about the bit in between?' asks Otto. 'The bit where the Russian soldiers arrive in our village?'

It's an important question.

We lie side by side, silent, staring up at the dark ceiling. What about the bit in between?

CHAPTER 9

O pen up! Quickly!' Someone is thumping on our front door, and the church bells are ringing even though it's not Sunday.

We all rush from the kitchen into the parlor. Opa unlocks the door and a German soldier barges in, coughing and wheezing as he brushes snow from his head and shoulders. He is almost as old as Opa and one of his hands is missing.

'The Russians are coming!' he shouts. 'The Red Army has broken through German lines. Their tanks are rolling across East Prussia, and they'll be here at any moment. You must leave immediately!'

I stare out the parlor window and see other soldiers running along the street through the heavy snow. They are the soldiers with gray hair and limps and uniforms that are too big. They are knocking at doors, pointing, yelling, ordering people to leave.

Yesterday, fleeing was forbidden. But now that it's too late, we're allowed to run away. *Commanded* to run away. In the middle of a blizzard. It doesn't make sense.

The church bells ring on and on.

'Child!' The soldier shakes my shoulder with his gloved hand. 'Did you hear me? You must help your mama now. Get away from here. Save yourselves.'

Save ourselves? As he leaves, I stare at his back in disbelief. Of course the Russians will be mean. They'll be angry. They might shout at us. They might even smash our windows or kick in our doors. But worse than that? No! We are not soldiers, just children and women and old men like Opa.

But Mama seems to believe him. 'Oh no! No! No!' she sobs. Her beautiful face crumples, then turns as white as the snow that is growing deeper and deeper outside our house. 'We should have fled. We should have disobeyed Hitler and the Nazi leaders and packed our bags and bought a horse and sleigh and left days ago.'

'We should have packed our bags and fled after Liesl was born, when this mess first began!' snaps Opa.

I was born in 1933, the same year that Adolf Hitler became chancellor. What is Opa saying? Our life has been good. *My* life has been happy.

I open my mouth to defend our glorious leader, to remind Opa of all Adolf Hitler has done for Germany, making us rich and healthy and the most powerful nation on earth. But Otto speaks first.

'Hitler is a worm,' he growls. 'He has lost our papa, and other people's papas and big brothers, and now he has left us all alone to fight the Red Army in the middle of a terrible blizzard. He hasn't even sent anyone to help us. Little Mia is just a baby, and there's nobody left to protect her from the soldiers and their guns and tanks.'

He pauses and jumps to his feet. 'Except me! I will keep Mia safe!' He scoops Mia into his arms and runs out of the parlor and upstairs.

'Otto is right,' says Opa. 'We are on our own. We can't expect that anyone is coming to help us. We must pack. Quickly.' He turns to Mama. 'Anna, you and Liesl must get all the warm clothes and bedding that you can fit into our trunk. Then fill the suitcases with anything else important.' He grabs Oma's hand. 'And you, my dear, must pack food. Everything we have. We'll need enough for weeks, maybe longer.'

Oma squeezes Opa's hand and disappears into the kitchen.

Opa pulls on his coat, scarf, and hat. 'I'm going out. I'll be back as soon as I've found transport.'

Mama and I lug our trunk and two suitcases from the basement up to the parlor. I dash upstairs to gather blankets, quilts, and eiderdowns. When I return with the first load, Mama is packing her finest dinner plates and a pretty silver sugar bowl. After the eiderdowns go in, she pops the mantel clock, a crystal vase, two brass candlesticks, and the family photo album on top.

When the trunk is full, we dash upstairs, and Mama fills the suitcases with her clothes—a fox stole, a pretty pleated skirt, two silk blouses, and her best dress. It's a green party dress, with a skirt made full and fluffy from layers and layers of black tulle.

'Mama,' I say, 'what about the diapers? Mia will need diapers.'

'But there's no room,' says Mama. 'The suitcases are full!' Her eyes are bulging with panic.

I reach into the suitcase, pull out her party dress, and hang it back in the wardrobe.

'Oh, Liesl. You are right.' Mama shakes her head. 'Why did I pack a party dress? It's just so hard to know what we will need. What we should leave behind . . .' She reaches out and presses the palm of her hand against my cheek. 'You are such a good, sensible girl, Liesl. I know I can always depend on you.'

I feel proud and smile at Mama. 'Anyway, it will all be here when we return,' I say.

Mama frowns, opens her mouth as though to speak, then closes it again. She makes herself busy filling the suitcase with Mia's diapers.

I gather the things I want from my bedroom—my schoolbooks, a clean handkerchief, a spare pair of socks and underclothes for both Otto and me. Otto will be too busy packing his toy airplane and cursing Adolf Hitler to think about clean underclothes.

When I return to Mama's room, she is emptying her jewelry box onto her bed. For a moment I think she is packing for fine parties again, but she isn't. She divides the earrings, rings, brooches, and bracelets into four small piles, then sews one of the piles into the lining of my coat, and another into the waistband of her skirt.

'For safekeeping,' she says. 'This way, the jewels will be secure and hidden from thieves.'

We will be all right, I think. *We are well prepared. Opa will soon return with a sleigh lined with comfortable cushions and thick rugs. And Oma will make us one last hot, hearty meal before we leave so our tummies are full. Everything will be all right.*

Mama dresses me, Otto, and Mia in all our winter clothes, one layer over the top of another so we can hardly bend our arms and legs. It is minus four degrees Fahrenheit outside, and we will need all the protection we can get. I am wearing two dresses, a cardigan, three pairs of tights, a scarf, a woolen hat, mittens, my mismatched boots, and my coat with the jewels sewn inside.

Mia's arms stick out sideways. She waves them about awkwardly, shouting, 'Tuck! Tuck!' She means she is stuck.

Mama takes one last look at her beautiful fur coat hanging in the wardrobe, then shrugs into Papa's coat—an old gray woolen thing that is far too big.

Opa clumps up the stairs and into the room. 'I bought a horse and cart from the Wagners. It's outside. Let's go.'

He and Otto take the suitcases. Oma shuffles in, awkward

under her many layers of clothing, and takes Mia's hand. I am about to follow them downstairs when Mama grabs me.

'Liesl, you must promise me something.'

'Of course, Mama.'

'Promise that if anything happens to me, you will keep Otto and Mia safe. No matter what, you must keep your brother and sister by your side. Don't let anything or anyone separate you.'

I step back as though I've been struck. 'Mama,' I whisper. 'Why are you asking such a thing?'

Mama seizes my hands. 'Promise me, Liesl.' She squeezes my fingers until they hurt. 'Promise!'

'Yes! Yes!' I shout. I want to say that it's a pointless promise. But I can't. The fear in Mama's eyes spreads to my heart, and I cannot speak another word.

Mama wraps her arm around my shoulders, and together we walk downstairs, along the hallway, through the door, and out. Out into the blizzard.

HUNTED WOLVES

CHAPTER 10

We are not all right. We are not well prepared. We do not flee in a rug-lined sled with easy loads, full tummies, and settled minds.

Instead, Otto, Oma, Mia, and I are perched awkwardly on top of our belongings on the wagon. Every cobblestone on the street rattles the wagon wheels, which in turn rattle our baggage and our bones. Opa and Mama walk: Opa leading the horse, Mama dashing around the wagon, pushing at suitcases and baskets when they look like they're slipping off. The only comforting thing is the horse. His name is Mozart and he is large, white, and beautiful.

Snow is falling heavily and the air is dangerously cold. Mia begins to cry the minute we start moving, so I pull her onto my lap and wrap her in my arms, even though I just want to huddle into a ball to keep myself from freezing. The sharp edge of a suitcase presses into my thigh, but I can't move without leaning into Oma, and I'm afraid I will push her off the wagon and onto the icy road. If she falls, Mia and I might topple after her.

Otto is hungry. He reminds us that we left home without eating lunch and that the food is buried at the bottom of the wagon, out of reach. He reminds us over and over again. Soon my own tummy is rumbling. Even though my toes and fingers and nose are aching with the cold, and my thigh feels as though it's about to drop off, my stomach fights angrily for attention. If someone were to offer me carrots right now, I would eat ten!

Mozart plods along the street until we fall into line with a row of vehicles—wagons, sleighs, and farm carts. The Krugers pull in behind us on their tractor. We haven't seen a tractor for years. They must have been hoarding the petrol. I stare at Frau Kruger to see if she's wearing Mama's pearls, but it's impossible to see beneath her scarf and coat.

Some warm, dry folk stare at us through the windows of their homes as we pass, but most in our village are trying to leave. I wonder if we have made the right choice.

By the time we reach the main road, Mozart has slowed to barely a shuffle. It looks like everyone in East Prussia is on the move, trying to head west, away from the Red Army. The road is crammed with wagons, carts, and sleighs pulled by horses, their loads piled high and wobbling like ours. There are hundreds of people walking, too, some pushing strollers and wheelbarrows and handcarts, some pulling small sleds, others carrying suitcases or bundles on their backs. Nobody was prepared for this.

Mia stops crying, and Mama begins to worry. She climbs aboard the wagon, taking the last bit of space, and stuffs Mia inside her coat. Now I understand why she brought Papa's baggy old coat and not her own snug-fitting fur. Mia will be warmer tucked inside against Mama's body.

We pass an old woman hobbling along with a walking stick. I am about to ask Opa to stop the horse and let the old woman climb up onto our wagon, but ahead I see two more old people with walking sticks, an old man being pushed in a wheelbarrow, little children crying, and dozens of mamas carrying babies. We can't help them all. We can't even help *one* because our wagon barely has room for Otto, Oma, Mia, Mama, and me. And surely Opa will need a rest soon. He is an old man himself.

I feel a sudden ache in my chest that is worse than the hunger in my tummy.

We trundle on, cold, hungry, scared, stunned. Sometimes everything comes to a halt—for minutes, or for what seems like an hour—and then we lurch forward once more. Animals that should be tucked safely away in their stables run wild across the fields—cows, pigs, horses, and goats.

For a while, a large spotted pig trots alongside our wagon, grunting up at us.

'I'm sorry,' says Otto, peering down at the pig. 'We don't

even have room for a mouse, let alone an enormous pig like you. I'm sorry!'

The pig leaves our side and trots away across the field.

Otto bursts into tears.

'It's all right, Otto,' I say, hugging him into my body so he can't see the tears pooling in my own eyes. 'The pig will be fine. In fact, he's probably happy. If he stayed at home, he'd be made into sausages, but now he's running toward freedom.'

'Where's freedom?' asks Otto.

I don't know where freedom is. I thought East Prussia was freedom. Germany was freedom. But now we are running away. Like rabbits from a fox. Like pigs from a sausage factory.

We pass wagons and carts with broken wheels that have been pushed off the road and into the gutter. Their loads are toppled, deserted. Suitcases spill their contents for everyone to see—shirts, skirts, dolls, books, bits of under-wear that are usually kept hidden from sight. There are empty strollers, broken wheelbarrows, snow-covered trunks.

There is even a grand piano, its once-beautiful timber now piled high with snow. An old man, half dazed, his beard caked in ice, leaves the road, lifts the lid, and plays a tune on the keys until the strings inside start to twang and snap. Another old man, with a double bass strapped to his back, grabs him by the arm and draws him back onto the road.

They are joined by two women: a short, plump one carry-

ing a piano accordion; another, tall and thin, carrying a violin. Together they wander on, singing the unfinished piano
tune. It is a good thing to see—and hear. A burst of music and
caring and light.

As the day draws on, Opa starts talking about shelter. He
leads our wagon from the road to a farm. He knocks on the
farmhouse door and chats with a woman, who nods and
points to the barn. She passes Opa an oil lamp and a can of
milk, and Opa passes her something from his pocket. Money?
It shimmers, and I realize it's his gold fob watch, a precious
family heirloom that he usually keeps tucked away with his
handkerchiefs and socks.

Opa returns smiling, his eyes shining in the lamplight, as
though he has just made the best deal of his life. He unhar-
nesses Mozart and leads him into the barn, telling us to unpack
the wagon and follow.

I suppose we will leave our luggage in the barn with
Mozart and his bucket of oats and go to the farmhouse to
sleep. I feel warmed by the thought of a roaring fire, a bowl
of steaming-hot soup, and a cozy dry bed in the attic. But
Mama starts spreading a blanket on the straw beside Mozart
and pulling out bits of food, and I realize that this is our home
for the night.

Soon, there are other people sharing our space. They
shuffle in, silent and weary, and set up their own little homes
in the stalls amid the cows and pigs. I wonder how much they

have paid the greedy woman for their shelter—a silver spoon, a gold bracelet, a diamond brooch? Anger pricks at my body.

Mama passes us each a chunk of rye bread, a cold boiled potato, and a slice of cheese, then pours a cup of milk each for Otto, Mia, and me. It's a strange supper, but we all eat hungrily, silently. Except for Oma. She breaks her food into little pieces and shares it between Otto and me.

'I'm not hungry,' she says. 'Old ladies like me don't need to eat all the time.'

Opa goes outside and returns with icicles he has broken from the eaves of the barn. 'To suck on when you are thirsty,' he explains.

I scrunch my nose, then realize he is serious. There is no water, only ice.

When we have eaten, Mama makes a nest in the straw using all of our blankets and eiderdowns. We huddle together like baby chicks, and Mama sings lullabies until Mia falls asleep in her arms. Oma falls asleep too.

'Look!' cries Otto. 'It's the musicians!'

The two old men and the two women who sang on the road come straggling through the barn door. They flop into the straw and moan. We wait for them to bring out blankets and food, but they have nothing more than their instruments. They look hungrily at Mozart's oat bucket and the pigs' trough.

I open our basket and take out a chunk of bread and some cheese.

'No, Liesl,' says Mama. 'We need to save what little we have.'

Opa rests his hand gently on Mama's shoulder. 'Anna, let her go. It is so very sweet, a great kindness that will far outweigh our loss.'

Mama nods, and I creep across the barn, past three cows and two other groups of travelers, until I am standing before the musicians.

'Hello,' I say. 'My name is Liesl. I saw you on the road.'

The tall, thin woman nods. 'Hello, Liesl. It is good to meet you. I am Maria. And these are my friends, Vera, Herbert, and Max.'

The other musicians smile, but there is no warmth, no energy in it.

I break the bread and cheese apart and hand it out. 'I liked your singing,' I say. 'It was very beautiful.'

Maria nods for me to sit with them while they eat. Normally, I'd think this was boring, but after seeing so many strange and terrible things today, it's lovely to watch something as simple as four people chewing. I don't even mind seeing all the crumbs gather in Herbert's beard. I think how nice it would be for a little mouse to live in there, all snuggly warm amid the hair with a grand supply of bread for nibbling.

When they are done, Vera, the short, plump woman, smiles, and I stand to leave.

'But wait!' cries Max. He pulls his double bass out of its

case and holds it upright, ready to play. 'A good meal must be paid for.'

The other three musicians shuffle about. Vera straps her piano accordion over her shoulders. Herbert brushes the biggest crumbs from his beard, pulls a piccolo from inside his coat, and stares at it. Maria tunes her violin. They find milking stools and an upturned bucket for seats, and soon they are arranged in front of me with their instruments, as if they were on a stage.

'For our new friend, Liesl!' announces Max, and he bows. He taps his foot four times, and the musicians launch into a cheerful dance tune.

My heart gives a little skip of surprise and I feel a smile stretch across my cold face.

Otto runs over, and we begin to dance, shyly at first, then with more energy as we find the rhythm and forget that we are being watched.

Other travelers leave their nooks and join us. Nobody speaks, but feet tap and smiles twitch. One by one they join in the dance, and soon there is a crowd, whirling, hopping, skipping, even singing.

The chill leaves our fingers and toes, and when the third tune begins, faster than the last, coats are peeled off, and cheeks start to glow. We leap around and around the barn, linking arms with strangers, bowing and smiling, until we have created a gathering of friends.

And we laugh! Even after such a day. Laughter and music

float up to the rafters and fill the barn with light and life and joy.

When the music ends, there is hugging and back-slapping, and people return to their own little nooks. The barn has changed. It is now a place filled with happiness and goodwill. And for the first time since leaving home this morning, I feel safe.

Opa beckons to the musicians. 'Come, come. We have enough blankets to share, and we have a baby who snores so loudly she will drown out any fearful sounds in the night.'

I watch as Mama and Opa make our new friends comfortable. We have so little, and yet this evening has been one of the happiest I can remember for a long time.

I think of the woman alone in her comfortable farmhouse just yards away, and now I feel nothing but pity for her.

CHAPTER 11

When I wake, the musicians and all the other travelers are gone. Opa has milked one of the cows and has warm, creamy milk waiting for us all. Oma doesn't eat. She sits in the corner, wrapped in an eiderdown, wheezing.

'Liesl,' says Mama, 'come and help me.' She opens our luggage and hands me one item after another, saying, 'Throw it away.'

At first, I sit things carefully down on the barn floor—the silver sugar bowl, the mantel clock, the crystal vase, the dinner plates, the brass candlesticks.

'I don't know what I was thinking,' Mama mutters. 'What good is a clock or a crystal vase when the world is crumbling around us? Stupid . . . stupid . . .'

But then, as she carries on sorting, she starts to shout, louder and louder, 'Throw it away! Throw it away!'

So I really start throwing, and Mama does too, and Otto runs over and joins in the game. Our schoolbooks fly across the barn, the pages flapping like wings before they plummet into a pile of manure. Mama's skirts and fine stockings and silk blouses drift through the air and catch on rakes and railings and nails poking from the walls. The fox stole lands on a cow, falling around her shoulders so that she looks like a fine dame heading out to the theater.

Opa walks by with Mozart, stops, bows to the cow, and sings, 'Delighted to meet you, Fräulein.' The cow bellows in reply and we all laugh.

The family photo album is harder to let go. Mama hugs it to her chest while Opa prepares the wagon. Taking out three photos, she tucks them into her pocket, then slips the album gently beneath a pile of hay.

'We can come back and find it one day,' I say.

'But not our schoolbooks,' says Otto. 'They're full of poo. And I don't just mean the muck from the pigs and cows!'

Now there's room in the wagon for Mama and Opa at the front. Opa takes the reins, and we try to return to the main road, but it's full of German Army vehicles—trucks, jeeps, and tanks—and hundreds and hundreds of German soldiers. The soldiers are silent, even their footsteps muffled by the snow.

Everyone is so quiet. Except for Otto.

'They're going the wrong way!' he shouts. 'The Russians are back that way! Go back! Go back! Go back and fight for Germany!'

He stands up in the wagon and flies his toy airplane through the falling snow, dropping imaginary bombs on imaginary Russians, as though this will show the soldiers what must be done.

A truck pulls up in front of us. An officer leans from the window. 'This road is for the military,' he shouts. 'We are retreating. I am sorry, but there is no room for civilians.' He waves across the field. 'You must go that way and join the next road.'

We stare across the snow-covered field to a forest.

The officer gets out of his vehicle. I hold my breath. Is he going to yell at us?

But when he reaches our wagon, he holds out a block of chocolate. 'I have a daughter your age,' he says to me. 'Be safe. Travel fast. The Russians are close.'

We head back the way we came, past the farm, then across the fields. The snow has formed deep drifts and is up to Mozart's flanks in places. He whinnies and grunts and blows steam from his nose. Poor thing, he must be cold and tired and hungry. Just like us. Maybe worse, because he is doing all the work.

The wheels of our wagon stick. Mama, Opa, Otto, and I climb down and push. Mozart tosses his head and rolls his eyes and surges on. He is a good German horse, brave and hardworking.

Late in the afternoon, we reach the next road and mingle in with the crowds—more wagons, sleighs, carts, and so many people on foot. All are silent. Nobody has energy for anything except keeping their blood flowing and plodding forward.

The snow falls heavily, on and on. Mama wraps Oma in an eiderdown, like a bratwurst in a bun, the sort we used to eat before meat became hard to find. Otto, Mia, and I huddle beneath a quilt. We peer out through the smallest gap we can manage.

'Look, Liesl!' cries Otto. 'There are so many things by the side of the road. Clothes and pillows and a sewing machine! More broken wagons. And a car!' He turns to me, eyes wide. 'Who would leave a car behind?'

'A car is useless without fuel,' I say. 'Just like Mozart would be useless if we had no oats for him to eat.'

Suddenly, Mama jumps off the wagon and runs to a trunk that has been tossed away. She opens the lid and pulls out a quilt.

'Mama!' I gasp. 'That's stealing!'

'But the owners left it behind,' says Mama. 'And this quilt is thick and dry. It can sit beneath the damp one that is over your heads. It will keep you warm.'

'But it's stealing!' I shout. 'Mama! We are not thieves.'

Opa turns to me, frowning. 'Liesl, enough! Your mama is right. There are times when it's all right to break the rules. *This* is one of those times.'

I take the quilt and glance around at the stream of people in front of and behind us, but no one takes any notice of

Mama's theft. In fact, others are doing the same—rummaging through abandoned luggage for food and blankets and warm dry clothes to replace the ones that have grown damp, then turned to ice against their bodies.

Two women are arguing over a pair of boots. One pushes the other so she falls to the ground, then they both start to cry. Mamas behaving like babies! I don't like it when the rules are broken.

Mia and Otto don't like it either. Their eyes boggle, and Mia's bottom lip is wobbling. I tuck them beneath my arms and pull the quilt in tight until they disappear.

'There, there, my little ducklings,' I say. 'You are safe and warm now beneath the mama duck's wings.'

Otto wriggles, but I won't let him out because now I can see something worse than mamas breaking the rules. There are mamas who have given up. They've slumped down by the side of the road with their children, and they are not getting up again. If they don't get up and keep walking, they will soon be covered in snow.

I tug the quilt in even tighter and start to sing Mia's favorite nursery rhyme, 'All My Ducklings.' My voice wobbles because it wants to cry, not sing. But the second time around, my words grow a little stronger.

Beneath the quilt, I hear Otto mumble along and then I feel Mia's little hands making beak actions. So I keep singing, over and over and over again. We paddle back and forth across the springtime lake with the ducklings, leaving behind the snow and the scattered luggage and the mamas who have forgotten how to behave and the thought that we are getting farther and farther from home with every step.

That night we find shelter in a church at the edge of a village, along with dozens more travelers. Mozart and the other horses must come inside too, for there is no shed or barn, but nobody complains. More bodies means more heat, and a horse is as good as four people at least.

We make our nest and eat our supper of bread and cheese. This time there is no rollicking dance tune from piccolo, double bass, piano accordion, or violin. Rather, there is the boom from cannons and rocket launchers in the east. Some are so close that the windows rattle and people catch their breath in fear.

Oma coughs and wheezes, and Opa rocks her back and forth like Mama does with Mia. I want to ask if Oma is all right, but I don't want to hear the answer.

Oma coughs, the rockets boom, the windows rattle, and Otto starts cursing Hitler beneath his breath. It is only a matter of minutes before he explodes and shouts something truly dreadful, and then where will we be? There are so many people in the church, and they will all hear Otto's traitorous words.

There is another boom that sends plaster crumbling from the ceiling.

Otto springs to his feet in fright and fury and shouts, 'Hitler is a—'

'Chocolate!' I cry. 'I forgot that we have a whole block of chocolate.'

I pull the chocolate from my coat pocket, and Otto sits down, his hand already open. Adolf Hitler is forgotten . . . for now.

Opa tells us about the first box of chocolates he ever gave Oma. 'The box was shaped like a heart and had at least a dozen chocolates inside—truffles, pralines, marzipan. Oma ate the whole lot while we sat on a bench in the Tiergarten in Berlin. And I thought, *Goodness, this woman can enjoy life! I think I would like to marry her and keep her by my side forever.*'

Oma smiles through blue lips.

Otto gobbles his chocolate, then Mama passes him her share. Anything to keep him quiet.

Mia grins and coos and dribbles chocolate down her chin. 'Mia love. Yum, yum.'

I smile. 'So many words. Mia is so clever!'

Mia claps her hands and shouts, 'Mia want!'

I look at the last square of chocolate in my hand and pass it to her. She sucks on it until it has melted, half in her mouth, half on her hands. Then she pulls off her woolen hat and rubs her fingers through her hair, her golden locks turning brown and sticky.

We laugh. The people beside us laugh too, and for a moment they feel like friends. It is a little spark of happiness in this sad, dark place.

CHAPTER 12

It's morning, and we should be on the road, but Oma is still sleeping, and Opa is making Otto and me recite the full name—first, middle, and last—of every family member we have ever met. Even Uncle Fritz, who smells like bacon and hates children.

'What's your name?' Opa quizzes again. 'Liesl!' I say, and roll my eyes.

'Ot-tohhh,' drones Otto. 'Can I play with your false teeth now, Opa?'

'No, no!' growls Opa. 'Concentrate! You are Liesl Anna Wolf and Otto Friedrich Wolf and Mia Hilda Wolf, the children of Erich Friedrich Wolf and Anna Edith Wolf. You are Wolfs, remember. Wolfs! Never *ever* forget it!'

Then Opa takes two of the photos Mama saved from our family album and makes us stick them inside our clothing, right down into our underwear. These are strange things to do, and I wonder if Opa is going a little bit crazy.

We feed Mozart, eat breakfast, and are made to recite the family names all over again. Still, Oma sleeps on, and Opa hasn't packed up his bedding.

'We are ready to leave,' whispers Mama. She kisses Opa and hugs him. Twice. The second time longer than the first—like a farewell.

'Mama!' I say. 'What are you doing?'

'Oma and I are staying here,' says Opa. 'You are going on without us today.'

'No!' I shout. 'We are family. We stick together.' I look to Mama, but she avoids my eyes.

Opa smiles and waves his hand in the air. 'You go ahead. Mozart is slow. We can catch up in a few days when Oma has had a rest. Maybe we can get a ride in a truck—travel in comfort and style.'

His voice is cheerful, but I can hear the ring of storytelling in his words. It is the same voice Mama uses for fairy tales. The same voice I used with Mia and Otto yesterday when I pretended to be their mother duck.

'Come, Liesl.' Opa's voice turns soft and low. 'Kiss your oma, then give your silly old opa a hug.' His eyes are pleading.

I crouch beside Oma and kiss her on the cheek. She doesn't wake up.

I stand and hug Opa. Tightly. Otto and Mia join us. We

are an Opa-Liesl-Otto-Mia blob, and for a moment it feels perfect.

Then Opa lets go.

The road is different today. The silence is gone. A worried murmur ripples through the fleeing crowds. There is the constant *boom-boom-boom* in the distance—cannons, guns, rockets. We see plumes of smoke making their way up into the sky, even flames.

'Moke!' says Mia, smiling. 'Boo! Boo!'

She is so proud that she knows what to call the smoke and the sound. I am sad that these are the words she must learn.

Otto keeps peering at the road behind us in case Oma and Opa are running to catch up.

'Perhaps they'll find a horse they can ride,' he says. 'Or a car that still has a little bit of petrol. Or one of those bicycles for two people that we saw at the beach that time!'

I nod and force a smile onto my face. 'Maybe.'

We enter a pretty village. It's a little like home, with its tidy brick cottages snuggled along a narrow street, but there's no sign of life. No cats. No dogs. No animal sounds coming from barns. No people peering from the windows. And it smells strange.

We turn a corner and stare in disbelief. The cottages in this street have holes in the walls. Big chunks of brick have been blasted away. Doors and windows have been ripped off and tossed into the street. Tables, chairs, beds, wardrobes, bookcases—all have been pulled out of the houses and scattered across the gardens. Not just scattered. Broken to pieces, their splinters sticking out of the snow like broken bones.

Through gaping doorways, we can see crockery, paintings, mirrors, jars of preserved fruit, all smashed. Books torn and trampled with muddy boots. Eiderdowns slashed, their feathers blanketing the floors like snow.

Otto grabs my hand and squeezes. 'Who would do such a thing?' he asks.

I have no answer. This is senseless. I can understand stealing, but this is crazy. *Nobody* can use these things again. As we continue through the village, the destruction worsens. Whole buildings have been blown up or burned to the ground.

'The Russians have been here already!' shouts a woman in the cart ahead of us. 'We are overtaken. There is nowhere to run!'

'Mama, what do we do?' I ask. 'Why are we running away if the Russians are already here? We should go back to Oma and Opa.'

'No,' says Mama. 'We carry on. Opa said we should head for the Vistula Lagoon. There are ships waiting in the Baltic Sea that will take us all to safety—west along the German coast, or even up to Denmark.' She pauses. 'It doesn't matter where. Just as long as it's away from here.'

'But here is East Prussia,' I say. 'Here is home.' Mama doesn't answer.

◄◄-►►

We travel on through farms—some broken like the village, some still whole. When poor Mozart starts to stumble, we stop for the night. We find a farm where there is room for us in the house. Tonight we will have real walls and ceilings and rugs on the floor. There might even be hot food.

Otto and I unharness Mozart. I take care to remember where all the straps and buckles go so I can hook him up again in the morning. We lead him into a stable that is clean and orderly and filled only with animals. There are no people.

Mozart snuffles and tosses his head. He seems glad to be in a proper barn once more. He too must be tired of things being a jumble. People living like animals. Animals going to church like people.

I lead him to a stall where there's a small donkey to keep him company, and give him food and water.

'Thank you for being a good horse,' I whisper. 'You have worked hard and kept us safe.'

I rub his soft white muzzle, then plant a kiss there. And, just like that, my heart feels a little spark of joy once more. Musicians. Babies with melted chocolate hair. Faithful horses. They are all treasure.

'Welcome! Welcome!' Herr Roth opens the door wide for us to come inside.

It's unusual to see a farmer at home, but Herr Roth is missing one leg, so he can no longer serve as a soldier.

'Welcome! Welcome!' sings Frau Roth, and she hugs each one of us as we walk into her kitchen.

Little children run in and out of the room, shouting and laughing, peek-a-booing and making faces at Otto and Mia, as though there is no war and the Russians have not broken through German lines and we have not left Oma and Opa behind. I think there are five of them, but they never stay still long enough to be counted.

Frau Roth has a giant pot of soup bubbling on the stove and four loaves of bread lined up on the table. There is even butter. Rich yellow butter!

Mama holds out her gold brooch. 'Payment,' she says, 'for our food and bed.'

But Frau Roth waves it away. 'No, no. A cuddle from the baby is payment enough.'

She holds out her hands and Mia toddles toward her. 'Yum yum?'

Frau Roth sweeps Mia into her arms and laughs. 'Of course. You must all be hungry.'

We squash around the table, slurping soup. We are too tired to talk, but it doesn't matter because the Roth children shout and laugh and yell enough for two families.

They are shouting and yelling and laughing so much that no one hears boots stomping through the farmyard. We barely even notice when the door flies open. We only jump in fright when a gun is fired and bits of wood splinter from the ceiling.

CHAPTER 13

Two Russian soldiers are pointing their weapons at us.

They're confused, I think. *We're just children. Any moment now they'll see and put their guns away.*

The soldiers walk around the table, staring into each of our faces. They keep their guns raised.

My heart thumps. They are *not* confused. They are angry.

Even though we are children, babies, women, and a one-legged farmer, we are Germans and they do not like us.

My hands shake. I slide them off the table and into my lap, but the younger soldier yells at me so I put them back where he can see them.

The older soldier shouts. We do not answer. We do not move.

He shouts even louder and sweeps three soup bowls off the table with the barrel of his gun. Soup splashes up my leg, soaking through my stockings, but I don't cry out. I don't dare make a sound.

The soldier drags Frau Roth to her feet and pushes her against the wall. He waves his gun at the rest of us.

'He wants us to line up,' says Herr Roth.

So we do, quickly, shaking, pressing our backs to the wall.

I hug Otto hard, as though my skinny arms are some sort of shield against the guns. Mama is doing the same to Mia, trying to hide as much of her little body in her arms and beneath her chin as she can.

The eldest Roth girl is weeping. Two of the little boys are huddled together, and the two little girls are clinging to the bottom of Frau Roth's skirt. Herr Roth is tottering on one leg without his crutches, his eyes darting back and forth between his children and Otto, Mia, and me. I can see he is worrying. There are too many girls and boys. How can he keep us all safe at once?

'Uri! Uri! Tick-tick! Tick-Tick!' shouts the oldest soldier.

I don't understand, but Herr Roth does. He hops over to the kitchen dresser, takes his watch from one of the drawers and passes it to the soldier.

The soldier holds the watch to his ear and grins. 'Tick-tick-tick-tick,' he says, his eyes shining like those of a child who has just been given a new toy. He pulls up his sleeve and his arm is *full* of men's watches! He adds Herr Roth's watch to the row.

Herr Roth hops back to his wife, and the young soldier smirks. He tilts his head to one side and stares at Herr Roth's bundhose. He steps forward and plucks at the leather pants. He runs his dirty fingers up and down behind the suspenders and pokes at the finely embroidered yoke. Then he narrows his eyes and shouts something in Russian. It sounds like a command.

Herr Roth doesn't understand. None of us understand. The soldier shouts louder, then pulls one of the suspenders of Herr Roth's bundhose down off his shoulder.

'He likes your pants!' I cry. 'He wants your bundhose.'

The soldier steps back and grins at me. 'Bundy-hose?' he repeats.

My face burns but I nod. 'Bundhose.'

'Bundy-hose!' cheers the soldier, his face splitting with a grin.

'Bundy-hose!' cheers the second soldier.

'Bundy-hose!' the first soldier shouts and points at Herr Roth.

Herr Roth falls into a chair, pulling off his pants as quickly as he can.

The soldier snatches them and thrusts them into the air like a victory flag. 'Bundy-hose!'

He and his friend laugh and slap each other on the back and sing a strange Russian song that includes the words, 'Tick! Tick! Tick! Tick! Bundy-hose! Bundy-hose!' at the end of every verse.

Then they smile and wave at us as though we are their dearest friends, and they leave. Just like that!

Otto and I run to the window and stare at the soldiers as they swagger away into the night.

Otto's eyes are hard, not their usual Otto-soft-and-happy. 'I hate Russians,' he hisses. 'Almost as much as I hate Hitler.'

CHAPTER 14

In the morning, Otto and I harness Mozart and lead him outside. He squints into the wind, and I know he'd rather be back inside with the donkey, but he's a good German horse and he obeys.

The snow falls on and on, as though it's forgotten how to stop. I've never seen so much, on the ground or in the air.

Mama tucks Mia into the trunk lined with quilts—a nest for a baby duckling.

'Ready?' Mama asks me.

I nod.

'Good.' She sighs. 'We are almost at the Baltic Sea. People on the road are saying that the ships are still leaving every day. Soon . . . Soon we'll be safe.'

We travel on. Mozart plods slowly through the snow.

Exhausted and freezing, I drift in and out of sleep.

I have muddled dreams about all that has happened. I am running around my school, shouting, 'Uri! Uri!' and stealing everyone's watches and all the clocks from the classroom walls. Fräulein Hofmann is frowning at me from the window, where her tongue has stuck to the ice. I am at home in our kitchen, buying the ingredients for a cake from Oma—eggs and lard, butter and salt, milk and flour and saffron—paying for them with strings of pearls and gold brooches. Mia stands nearby, clapping and burbling the cake song, as Oma frowns and tells me I have paid too much. Too much! I am sitting in church and Mozart is standing in the pulpit, dressed as a priest, giving the sermon. He is far more interesting than our boring old priest.

Otto sleeps too, his head snuggled in my lap. He dribbles, and the dribble turns to ice and his cheek sticks to my coat. I doze and wake and shiver and ache and doze again, and I no longer know whether we have been fleeing for days or weeks or even years.

We reach the Vistula Lagoon in the middle of a blizzard. There are soldiers from the Wehrmacht, our glorious German Army, and our hearts leap for joy at the sight of them.

The soldiers tell us that the ships are waiting in the harbor at Pillau, seven miles away on the other side of the lagoon. The Russians are everywhere—to the north, the south, and the east—so the only way to get to the ships is straight across the frozen lagoon. There are weak spots and holes where the Russians have been firing rockets onto the lagoon, but there are no Russians out there on the ice.

'It's your best chance,' says a young soldier. His face is dirty and his uniform is tattered, but his eyes are soft and kind. 'We've marked a track with branches stuck into the ice. Follow the branches. But don't get too close to other travellers. Too much weight and the ice will crack.'

Mama squints through the falling snow and shakes her head. She looks like she wants to cry but has forgotten how. Or maybe the tears are freezing before they can fall.

I step forward and take her arm. 'A track across the ice where there are no Russians is a good thing, Mama!'

'What happens if the ice cracks?' asks Otto.

'You sink into the lagoon,' says another soldier.

'I can swim!' shouts Otto. 'I'm seven, and I swim like a fish.'

'Not here, you can't,' says the soldier. 'Even the fish freeze in these waters.'

Mama takes off her coat—Papa's old coat—and buttons it around Mia and me. Mia disappears into the Liesl-Mia-coat cocoon without a fuss. She has grown used to this strange new life. As long as she is hugged and fed, she doesn't grizzle. Is it normal for a baby to be so quiet? So uncomplaining?

It's not normal for Mia.

'Liesl!' shouts Mama. 'Did you hear me?'

I shake my head.

'Listen,' she snaps. 'We're almost there, but this is the most dangerous part of our journey. You must be ready for anything. You must protect Mia no matter what. And Otto, too. I'll be busy keeping Mozart and the wagon in the right place.'

I remember the promise Mama forced from me before we left home. My chest aches. My tummy lurches. But I nod.

Mama wraps a blanket around Otto like a shawl, and another around herself.

Mozart whinnies and wobbles on his legs.

'Not much farther, my friend,' says Mama, kissing his soft white muzzle. Although I suspect she is trying to soothe herself more than the horse.

We climb aboard the wagon and head out onto the ice.

It is strange on the frozen lagoon. The wind howls, and the snow blows sideways and in circles and sometimes back up into the sky. The branches that guide our way stick out of the ice like a forest of dead trees. I feel like we're caught in the pages of a fairy tale where the land has been cursed by a wicked witch and everything has frozen, and nothing good can ever happen again until the chosen one comes along and finds a golden orb or sings a special song. But there are no golden orbs out here, and a song would be lost on the wind.

'Liesl!' Otto grabs my arm. 'What's that?'

Just yards away, two pieces of wood poke from the ice. They are long and smooth and have metal rings and leather straps attached. There is something familiar about them.

I look past Mama to Mozart and let out a little cry, for I see the same two pieces of wood there—the drawbars of our wagon that are connected to Mozart's harness.

'It's nothing, Otto,' I lie, but at the same time Otto cries, 'It's a wagon! It's a wagon! Liesl! Liesl! Someone's wagon is frozen beneath the ice. It's frozen into the lagoon!'

He stares at me, his eyes big and round, and I know that, like me, he's wondering if there were people on board when the wagon broke through the ice. Are the people *still* there? The horse, too? Is everything, everyone, frozen in the ice?

I wrap my arm around Otto and he presses in so hard that I think he might push me off the wagon.

Travel is slow. Every time a group in front of us slows or halts, Mama is careful to stop at a distance from them.

The snow lightens, and at first it seems like a blessing, because we can see farther afield. I remember, years ago, Mama and Papa bringing us on a trip to this same lagoon. Otto was only tiny, so perhaps he can't remember, but I can recall every detail. It was winter, and the lagoon was frozen. The sun shone, and the sky was silver-blue. Ice yachts skated across the lagoon, gliding, zigzagging, weaving in and out of one another, their white sails like the wings of giant birds. Around the edges of the ice, hundreds and hundreds of people were skating. Mamas and papas were teaching their children to skate. Brothers and sisters chased one another, squealing and laughing. Girlfriends and boyfriends danced together on their skates, gliding about like princes and princesses at a grand winter ball. The air was humming with happiness. It was the most beautiful place I had ever been, and I cried when Mama and Papa said it was time to go home.

Now I'd give anything to leave. For the lagoon is no longer a place of beauty, but a scene of horror. Broken wagons and dead horses lie scattered across the ice, an explosion of shattered belongings around them. Many more wagons have sunk through the ice and frozen, with just a wheel, a post, a length of harness still visible above the surface. Ahead and behind, stretching out in an endless line of misery and fear, are the plodding travelers, all hoping to make it across the ice to the harbor where a magical ship waits to take them to safety.

I rock back and forth and don't realize that I'm whimpering until Otto starts hitting me.

'Liesl, stop! Stop! You're scaring Mia! You're scaring *me*!'

But it's not *me* who is scaring him. It's not! It's this nightmare! This place that is stuck in a fairy-tale curse.

I rock and wail and don't stop until a loud crack cuts through the air. Otto and I stare at each other.

There is a whistling sound above our heads, and farther along the convoy of wagons, we see something drop from the sky and fall through the ice. Ice and water explode upward.

Horses buck and rear, toppling their wagons. A cart slips backward through the hole in the ice, taking everything, even its horse, with it.

Horses try to bolt but slip on ice, bog in snow, stumble in

panic. People jump from their wagons and try to run to safety, but where will they go?

There are more loud cracks, more whistling sounds overhead, more explosions. We are under attack! The Russians are firing their artillery from the shores of the lagoon. They must *know* there are women and children and frail old men and kind, faithful, hardworking horses out here, and yet they fire shell after shell after shell.

Mozart bolts. He takes us flying across the ice, away from the path the soldiers have marked out. He gallops on and on, blinded by fear, driven by his instinct to survive, until a shell lands a little way ahead of us.

Mozart rears up and whinnies. He stomps about, rolling his eyes and flaring his nostrils.

Mama tries to control him, but she can't, and it doesn't even matter because the next shell blows a hole in the ice right near the back of our wagon.

I stare at the gaping circle of black water. I press Mia into my body with one hand and grab Otto's hand with the other.

The ice cracks and crumbles around the edge of the hole, crawling toward our wagon.

'Mama!' I scream.

'Jump! Run!' shouts Mama.

Another shell hits nearby, and the air is full of ice, water, screams, fear, kicking hooves, and splinters of wood. I don't know what I'm doing or where I'm going. I am blind and deaf and stupid with terror.

I drag Otto across the ice, running, crying, bumping into other people, a horse, a flying suitcase, a violin with its strings flapping free, and keep running. The shells keep falling, one after another, and I look back and I can no longer see Mozart or the wagon, but Mama said to run and to look after Mia and Otto, so I do. I run with impossible strength and I keep Mia pressed against my body and I drag Otto all the way. Sometimes he is running, sometimes he is sliding along the ice, begging me to stop, but I don't.

I don't know how long we run, or slide, or where we go, but finally we reach a forest, and I know that we have left the lagoon and are back on land.

But there is no harbor, no ship, no Baltic Sea across which we will sail to safety, and no Mama.

CHAPTER 15

We wait.

For Mama. For help.

For some idea about what we should do next.

Otto takes his toy airplane from inside his coat. He looks at it for a moment, then stands and throws it as far away as possible. It flies through the air, soaring between the trees, and disappears into a drift of snow. Missing in action.

The sun disappears. The snow starts falling heavily. And still we are all alone.

'Mama!' whines Mia from inside my coat. 'Want Mama!'

'I want Mama too,' whimpers Otto. 'Where is she, Liesl?'

'Mama . . . ,' I begin. 'Mama . . .' But I can't get the words out. What did I see? The wagon disappearing beneath the ice.

Mozart galloping away. But Mama . . . ? 'I don't know,' I say. 'I don't know.'

We'll freeze if we stay here.

'Come,' I say, dragging Otto to his feet.

'Where are we going?' he asks.

I don't answer. I brush the snow off our shoulders. Tighten our scarves. Act like I'm not scared. Pretend I have a plan. To keep Otto going. To keep myself going.

We press through the trees, knee-deep in snow, then waist-deep. Bodies numb. Hearts numb.

Just when I think we can't do this anymore, and the gray of day is being sucked into night, we come out of the trees and stumble across a farm. There's a large timber barn and a sturdy brick house.

Otto rushes ahead.

'Wait!' I cry. 'The German soldiers said there are Russians all around the lagoon. What if they're here in this house? What if they're like the soldiers at Herr Roth's farm?'

Otto gasps. 'What if they're *worse*?'

I shrug. We both know that we will have to settle for the barn.

I squeeze Mia to my chest, urging her to keep silent. We creep along the back wall and hear the swoosh and sweep of noses in straw.

'Cows,' whispers Otto.

'Dry straw,' I whisper back, and nod encouragingly.

How strange our lives have become! The chance to sleep with cows, even if the Russians are lurking just yards away, feels like a blessing.

We creep along the outer wall of the barn until we get to the door. But just as we're about to go in, I grab Otto by the arm and point toward the house.

'There's no light,' I whisper.

Otto is running across the open yard to the farmhouse before I can stop him. He crouches beneath a window, pops up like a jack-in-the-box, then flops down again.

Mia squirms and I rock her back and forth.

Otto pops up again and this time he wipes the snow away from the windowpane and peers in. He beckons for me to join him.

We creep around the house, peering in through every window. There's nobody there.

'Let's go in,' says Otto.

I stare at him. 'But that would make us burglars!'

Otto shrugs. 'I don't mind being a burglar.'

My eyelashes are thick with snowflakes, and I decide that I don't mind either.

Inside is warm and dry. I set Mia free at last, sitting her down in a soft, squishy armchair.

The charcoal from the last fire sits in the grate. Nobody has bothered to clean it away. Otto and I work silently, building a new fire—straw, twigs, then bigger logs when the flames are hot and hungry.

The house lights up enough for us to find candles and lamps, and we light them all.

We look around. This large room is parlor, dining room,

and kitchen all in one, with a bedroom off to the side. The ceilings are crossed with heavy timber beams and the floorboards are scattered with worn rugs. It's plain and comfortable, but there is something more. Something not quite normal.

This is a house frozen in time.

Knives and forks lie crookedly across plates that contain a half-eaten supper—casserole, mashed potato, sauerkraut. The end of a loaf of bread sits in the middle of the table, surrounded by crumbs. The pots on the stove are still dirty, their edges caked in gravy and mashed potato. There's tea in the cups, still waiting to be drunk.

A prayer book lies open beside the plate at the head of the table, a pair of spectacles resting on top. I wonder if they got to 'Amen.'

'The people who live here have run away!' says Otto. He shovels three forkfuls of cold mashed potato from one of the plates into his mouth.

'Perhaps the Russian Army took them by surprise,' I suggest. 'One moment they were safe and warm, enjoying their supper. The next they heard cannons and guns and rockets, so they ran.'

Otto looks around. 'But the Russians *didn't* come, did they? It's not like the houses in that village we saw. Nothing is trampled or ripped to shreds. No windows are smashed. No furniture has been tossed into the yard. No doors or shutters are torn off. Nobody has stomped on the books. Nobody has fired bullets into the walls or set fire to the barn.'

I shiver. 'No. The Russians must have passed by without finding this farm.'

'Lucky for us,' says Otto.

'Yes!' I agree. 'Lucky for us.'

I change Mia into a clean, dry diaper—or, at least, a clean dry towel that I pretend is a diaper.

Mia smiles and thanks me by pressing her soft little hands against my cheeks and saying, 'Mia love Lees.'

I kiss her on the cheek and hug her tightly. 'I love you too, Mia.'

It is a normal moment in this very strange day. A warm spark of joy that has survived the ice.

'Liesl! Mia!' shouts Otto from somewhere beyond the kitchen. 'I have a surprise for you!'

Mia toddles toward Otto's voice. I follow, and we find him standing in the middle of a well-stocked larder, a cheese wheel in one hand, a gherkin in the other. Both have enormous bites taken from them, and Otto's cheeks are bulging. He's like a squirrel with a mouth full of acorns.

'Food!' he shouts, spraying bits of green gherkin into Mia's hair.

There is *so much* food—three loaves of rye bread, five cheese wheels, a string of sausages, a leg of ham. How long has it been since we have seen this much meat all at once?

There are baskets of cabbages, potatoes, turnips, carrots, and apples. One shelf is packed with preserves—cherries, plums, pears, pickles, sauerkraut, blackberry jam, elderberry jelly. There's a pot of honey with honeycomb floating inside, a jar filled with almond biscuits, and a pat of butter as big as a brick.

'Yum yum!' shouts Mia, stretching out her hands.

Otto gives Mia the cheese wheel. She holds it in both hands and sucks on it. She dribbles and grins, then sits the entire cheese wheel on her head like a hat.

Otto and I burst out laughing, and Mia giggles along with the joke.

I open a jar of blackberry jam and eat it with a spoon. I open a second jar and hand it to Mia. She throws away her spoon and uses her hand to scoop out the deep-purple yum yums. Otto takes a bite of an apple, a bite of an almond biscuit, a bite of cheese, then starts all over again.

When the edge of our hunger is gone, we gather up our favorite foods and some plates from the kitchen and make a picnic beside the fire. We start with rye bread spread thickly with butter and jam. We eat wedges of cheese pressed between slices of ham. And we finish with preserved pears drizzled in honey.

Mia loves the honey—both for eating and rubbing into her hair. She gurgles and says, 'Yum! Yum! Yum!' over and over again, until finally she falls asleep with her head on a loaf of bread. She doesn't even need a lullaby.

Otto lies back on the rug, his head on a cushion, his hands patting his bulging belly.

I look at the dirty plates, the leftover food, and the honey-drizzled rug and feel a sudden pang of guilt. *Thieves,* I think. *We have become dirty thieves and vandals.*

And then a worse kind of guilt presses in on me. Where is Mama right now? Here we are, having a party, gobbling like pigs at a trough, and we don't even know what has become of Mama.

But then Mia rolls over so that her head slips off the bread. She snores and rubs at her hair in her sleep and looks grubby and happy and cuter than ever.

I look over to Otto. His eyelids are growing heavy, but the smile is still glued to his mouth.

Then I look back at the half-eaten almond biscuit in my hand. And I know that this is not a bad thing. We need to eat. We need to rest. We need to be children. Even in the middle of a war.

I promised Mama that I would take care of Mia and Otto. Today, I have done my job well.

CHAPTER 16

The next morning, we can hear the soft thud of cannon fire again, but the snow is still falling heavily, so we stay. Besides, where would we go? We don't even know where we are, or what lies beyond the farmyard and the ring of forest that surrounds us.

Otto presses his face against the window and stares at the barn. 'It looks like a gingerbread house with thick icing all over the roof.'

'Like in "Hansel and Gretel,"' I suggest.

'Yes!' He turns to me, his face alight as he recalls the fairy tale.

Otto is so easily lost in the moment. Dying of a broken heart. Seething, bubbling, boiling with anger. Gobbling his favorite foods. Beaming with happiness.

I join him at the window, my shoulder pressed against his,

and peer out at the gingerbread barn and the sugar-frosted forest beyond. It is a fairy-tale land that has been kept safe from the war that rages all around. But then I shudder and turn away, because even the most beautiful fairy-tale land has a wicked witch lurking somewhere nearby.

Mia waddles toward us, her golden hair standing on end.

She scrunches her nose. 'Mia wet.'

'Mia smelly!' cries Otto.

'Mia bath!' I shout.

We find a tub and drag it in front of the fire. It takes an hour to boil the water and fill the tub, but it's worth it. Otto's and Mia's faces grin up at me through the soap suds.

I try to pin each of them down to scrub away two weeks' worth of grit and grime, but they both wriggle and duck and squeal and splash like wild animals. Mia rubs soapy water into her hair until last night's honey is all gone. Her hair is still a tangle of knots, but at least they are clean knots.

I stoke the fire until the farmhouse feels like a furnace, and Mia and Otto run naked while I bathe. I soap and scrub and think how many times in my life I have bathed without realizing how amazing it is. Filth hurts. It works its way into the creases in your elbows and knees. It builds up under your fingernails and toenails, behind your ears, between your toes, in the crease beneath your chin. It presses and rubs and stings and makes you grumpy. But a bath is the miracle cure.

The photographs that were stuffed down our underwear

sit on the mantelpiece. Mama, Papa, Oma, and Opa smile down at me from one photo. Mama, Papa, Otto, Mia, and Liesl smile down at me from the other. I start reciting the family tree—first, middle, last names of everyone in the Wolf family—just as Opa made me on that last morning we were together.

Otto appears in the doorway from the bedroom. He's wearing a man's undershirt that reaches to his ankles and a pale-blue lady's hat with a bow on one side.

'I've found some clothes!' he cries. 'Lots of soft, clean clothes to keep us warm. Even children's clothes. They're all for boys, but you can pretend to be a boy.' He grins. 'I always wanted a big brother.'

I throw the cake of soap at him from the bath.

There is everything we need in the chest of drawers. The boys' clothes are just the right size for Otto and me.

'I like the feel of long johns and trousers,' I tell Otto. 'They're so much warmer than a skirt and tights.'

'I like this hat,' says Otto, putting the pretty blue hat back on his head once he's fully dressed.

I pull a sweater over Mia's head and roll up the sleeves to let her hands poke free. I tie a knit bonnet beneath her chin, kiss her cheek, and sing, 'Clean, warm clothes!'

'Stolen clothes!' shouts Otto, tilting the pretty blue hat at a jaunty angle.

'Not stolen,' I say. 'Borrowed.'

Otto scrunches his nose. 'So we'll give them back?'

I look down at the red sweater I'm wearing. It's thick and warm and so much cleaner than the one I peeled off before my bath.

I blush. 'No. We won't give them back.'

'So we *are* stealing,' says Otto. 'We're thieves. Again!'

I bite my lip. 'Just until the war is over,' I explain.

'How long will that be?' he asks.

'Soon. And when we get back home, we can buy some new clothes for the people who live here. We'll send them a parcel. It will be a kind of thank-you gift for letting us stay and for using all their things.'

Otto grins. He likes the idea.

I like the idea too, but I can't help feeling as if I've just told a terrible lie. A bundle of terrible lies.

I am a burglar, a thief, a vandal, *and* a liar.

I clean the kitchen and the dining table and make a hearty lunch of boiled potatoes, fried sausages, and bread with thickly spread butter.

I sit at the head of the table like the mama. 'Take your hats off,' I command.

Otto removes his and Mia's hats and sits on them.

I press my hands together and wait until Otto and Mia do the same. I close my eyes and say grace in my best poetry voice: 'Come, Lord Jesus, be our guest. May our meal be truly blessed.'

'Amen!' shouts Otto. Mia claps.

I serve up the food.

Mia eats and rubs butter and sausage grease into her hair. Otto eats and talks with his mouth full and laughs at Mia's greasy hair.

I slam my hand down on the table and scold, 'You children have despicable manners! You should be ashamed of yourselves.'

Otto burps.

Mia picks up a whole sausage and pokes it into her ear. I burst out laughing.

We chew with our mouths open and flap our elbows and scratch our bellies and flick food from our forks at one another and squeal until we run out of breath. We don't mention Mama or what happened on the ice. We don't wonder if Oma and Opa will suddenly catch up and appear on the doorstep, rubbing their wrinkled old hands and asking for a cup of coffee and an almond biscuit. We don't mention the family who own this house, or talk about why they have fled so suddenly, leaving everything behind—even their half-finished supper. We are playing a game. It's the Happy Family Game. It is every bit as unreal as the gingerbread house in 'Hansel and Gretel,' or the fountains flowing with lemonade, but every bit as wonderful. Because as long as we are lost in the game, we don't have to think about the real world.

After lunch we sleep again, this time in the double bed

piled high with eiderdowns. We wake, I cook more sausages, we eat, then we sleep all night long.

We need this time to rest from the journey we have taken.

We need this time to build up strength for the journey that lies ahead.

Wherever that might be.

CHAPTER 17

On the second morning, Otto wakes me. 'Liesl,' he hisses. 'There's a strange sound.'

I sit up, my heart thumping in my chest. 'What is it? Guns? Tanks? Soldiers creeping around outside?' I squeak. 'Soldiers creeping around *inside*?'

A long, low bellow drifts across the farmyard.

'It's coming from the barn,' says Otto. 'The Russian soldiers might be in there. Maybe they're being mean to the cows.'

My whole body begins to shake. 'We'll have to leave,' I whisper. 'Before they break into the house.'

'But I don't want to leave,' sobs Otto. 'I like it here. There's food, and it's warm and dry.'

The cow bellows again.

Otto howls. 'I don't want to leave, but I don't want the Russians to get me!'

Me neither.

'We'll sneak out and see what's happening,' I say. 'If there are soldiers, we'll hide in the forest, just until they're gone. Then we'll come back after dark.'

Otto nods.

We slip out of bed and into our clothes. Otto presses the pretty blue hat down over his knit woolen hat. Maybe he's too scared to think straight. Or maybe the hat makes him feel brave.

We wake Mia, change her diaper, and bundle her into her old coat and the stolen bonnet.

We hold hands—a Liesl-Mia-Otto line—and run through the farmhouse together. We are almost at the kitchen door when I stop. I look down at Mia and across to Otto. Do I take them with me, or do I leave them here, alone in the house?

It's just ten yards across the yard to the barn, but I know that the world can change in such a space. Ten yards. Ten seconds.

The bellowing sound reaches us once more. Otto shakes my arm. 'Liesl!'

I race into the larder and fill my pockets with chunks of bread and bits of cheese.

'All right,' I say. 'A quick dash to the side of the barn. A peek inside. If there's trouble, we'll run. Deep into the forest.' I sweep Mia up onto my hip and pass her a crust of bread. 'No talking.'

The yard between the house and the barn seems

enormous. My legs are moving as fast as they can go, but it takes far longer than ten seconds. It takes hours, weeks, years to get to the side wall where we're sheltered from sight once more.

I press against the timber and try to catch my breath without huffing and puffing out loud. The cow bellows again, but I don't hear any human sounds.

I pass Mia to Otto and creep along the wall until I find a crack. I press my eye to it and squint.

My legs wobble. I slide down the barn wall until I am sitting in the snow.

And I smile.

'It's all right,' I say. 'Everything is all right.'

We slip quietly into the barn. There are five fat caramel-colored cows. Four of them stare at us with soft brown eyes. The fifth is lying in the straw, nudging something brown and wet at her side.

'What's wrong with her?' asks Otto.

'Shhh,' I whisper. 'Come here and watch.'

I sit on a pile of hay. Mia crawls into my lap, and Otto nestles beside me.

The cow licks the wet bundle, and it moves. Otto jumps in fright. I reach out and squeeze his hand.

The cow licks, and the bundle wriggles and squirms and lifts its head.

'A calf!' shouts Otto, then slaps his hand over his mouth. He grins up at me and whispers, 'It's a newborn calf, Liesl.'

I nod and smile. Joy bubbles up inside my chest.

The cow stands and sniffs the calf. She licks it all over and nudges it with her nose. The calf wriggles and stretches. It stands for a second, then flops nose-first into the straw.

The cow lets out a soft, low murmur. It sounds like, 'Well done. Now try again.'

The calf tries again, and this time it staggers along for two steps before flopping down.

Mia reaches her hands out toward the calf. 'Mia love dog.'

Otto chuckles. 'It's not a dog! It's a calf. Mia loves the calf.'

The calf stands and wobbles and becomes more certain of its legs. The cow uses her head to guide it toward her udder, and the calf has its first drink of milk, tail wagging.

Mia gurgles with delight and grabs at the air. 'Mia love dog! Woof!'

'It's a calf!' says Otto. 'Moo! Moo!'

Mia stares at Otto. She turns back to the calf and cries, 'Mia love dog. Moo!'

Otto and I burst out laughing, and Mia jumps up and down, shouting, 'Moo! Moo! Moo!' thrilled at this new word she has learned.

The cow stares at us, then blinks down at her newborn calf as if to say, 'See what I have done. I have created the most beautiful thing on earth.'

And we all agree. The calf is a gift.

It's a magical gift that ties us to the farm.

We will stay and wait, and surely Mama will find us again.

Mama will find us, and she'll have the same love in her eyes as the cow has when she blinks at her calf.

'We should stay awhile,' I tell Otto that night when we go to bed.

'Good idea!' he cries. 'We can look after the cows.'

'Moo! Moo!' sings Mia, squirming between us.

'Mia's in love with the little calf,' I say.

'Yes,' Otto agrees. 'And if we left, she would miss him. She'd cry, and there'd be lots of tears and lots of snot. And then she'd blow her nose and rub the dirty hankie in her hair.'

We both laugh because it's just the sort of thing Mia would do.

Otto is silent for a long time, then he whispers, 'I was scared this morning, Liesl.'

'Me too,' I say.

'But I was really, *really* scared. Terrified and sick in my tummy and wobbling in my boots.'

'Me too!' I insist. 'It's all right to be scared, Otto. Even mamas and papas and opas get scared. You saw how frantic everyone was when we were fleeing from the Red Army.'

'But I thought I would be different,' he says. 'I thought I'd be brave, no matter what. Like in our bedtime stories and in the battles my friends and I held in the street. I really thought I'd be a hero. But I'm not brave, and I never *ever* want to be a soldier. I'm a coward. I didn't even stay behind to help Mama when the ice broke. I'm a stupid coward!' He bursts into tears. 'See? I'm blubbering even now!'

I reach out and stroke his head. 'You're *not* a coward, Otto. You're a normal seven-year-old boy. You don't have to be a brave soldier. You just need to be my precious brother, and Mia's precious brother. That's enough.'

Otto sniffs and his hand squeezes my fingers. 'Really?' he whispers.

'Really,' I reply. 'And for a little while, you might also need to be a cow farmer.'

Otto likes the idea. He wriggles a little closer, squashing Mia between us like a piece of cheese between two slices of ham.

'And your first job will be to give the new calf a name,' I say.

'Dog!' shouts Otto, with barely a thought. 'His name is Dog.'

'Yes, of course it is,' I reply.

'Dog,' says Mia. 'Moo! Moo!'

CHAPTER 18

Three more calves have been born. Otto, Mia, and I sit in the straw watching them.

'They need names,' says Otto. 'Dog has a name, so the others need names too.'

'Ginger,' I say, pointing at the calf that has an orange tinge to her hair.

'Perfect!' cheers Otto.

Mia claps and dribbles. She crawls toward Ginger, but I grab her by the foot and drag her back.

'No, Mia,' I say, tucking her into my lap. 'We're just looking, remember. No touching. The mama cows will worry if we go near their babies.'

Mia stares up at me, her blue eyes wide. 'Mia love dog,' she coos.

'I know,' I say. 'We all love the dogs—I mean calves. But

if we go near them, the mama cows might think we're going to hurt them. And when mama cows worry, they kick, or knock people over with their big fat heads, or poke with their long sharp horns.'

'Ouchies!' says Otto, frowning and rubbing his head to support my argument.

Mia jumps up and down in my lap, squealing.

One of the calves startles at the sound. He stumbles and falls over in the straw, then wobbles to his feet and runs to his mama.

'Wobbles!' cries Otto. 'That one should be called Wobbles.'

I smile. 'Dog, Ginger, and Wobbles. Now, Mia, *you* need to name the last calf.' I kiss my little sister on the head. 'What shall we call her?'

Mia stares up at me and smiles. 'Moo! Moo!'

'Good one!' says Otto. 'Dog, Ginger, Wobbles, and Moo!' And we all burst out laughing.

We spend hours in the barn each day. Otto works like a full-grown farmer, shoveling the muck away, spreading clean straw, making sure the troughs are full of water and hay. As he works, he sings little songs. I think this is rather sweet until I realize he's making up rude ditties about Hitler. But at least he's happy.

I spend a lot of time just sitting with Mia, watching. The calves are a miracle. Each one fills me with wonder. And they keep me from fretting. When I'm in the barn, I don't panic about Mama or wonder why she hasn't yet wandered out of the woods and into the farmhouse. I stop worrying about how quickly we are eating our way through the larder. I stop puzzling over the fact that our Führer, Adolf Hitler, hasn't yet beaten back the Russians. Even the distant cannon fire seems to fade to nothing, and all I can hear is mooing, murmuring, suckling, and Mia's excited squeals.

But now, suddenly, I realize the barn has grown silent.

I look about and my breath catches.

Mia is toddling toward Dog the calf. She's shuffling through the straw, reaching out her hands, opening and closing her fingers, preparing to grab the caramel ears, the brown eyelashes, the wagging tail—whatever she can reach first.

Dog's mama has stopped eating and is staring at Mia. 'Mia,' I whisper, my heart thumping.

But Mia keeps going, unaware of the danger.

The cow trots toward Mia and her calf, head down, letting out a low, menacing moo. Her horns seem longer and sharper than they were yesterday.

'Mia!' I shout, springing to my feet.

Mia turns and comes face to nose with the cow. 'Moooooo!' says the cow.

'Moooooo!' replies Mia, then she kisses the cow on her giant, slimy pink nose.

The cow blinks. Mia stares.

I hold my breath.

And then the cow licks Mia across the face.

Mia beams, then turns to Dog and wraps her arms around his neck. The calf dashes away and Mia falls over.

The mama cow trots to my little sister's side and nudges her. 'Get up! Get up!' she seems to be saying to Mia. 'You can do it, little one.'

And Mia does, and she toddles after Dog once more.

I watch in wonder as Mia runs around the barn with the calves, mooing, squealing, grabbing at tails and ears, and kissing, kissing all the time. Occasionally, a mama cow comes near to sniff or lick this strange new baby, and Mia kisses them too. Always in the middle of their slimy pink noses.

Finally, when Mia is satisfied that everyone has been cuddled and kissed and grabbed and squeezed and loved enough, she curls up in the straw with Dog and falls asleep. Soon her snores are rising up into the rafters, and she and Dog are joined by Ginger, Wobbles, and Moo.

The cows watch over all the babies with loving brown eyes. They've accepted Mia as one of their own.

Mia is safe and loved and happy. It's as though the cows are filling the gap where our own mama should be.

Otto is shaking my shoulder, pushing away the quilts.

'Liesl! Wake up! I can hear noises. The last cow must be having her baby. I want to watch!'

It's pitch-black, the middle of the night.

Mia sits up from her spot between us on the bed and rubs her eyes. 'Moo! Moo!' she murmurs, still half asleep.

I laugh. 'Let's go.'

We bundle up, light the oil lamp, and run across the yard to the barn. We are so excited about the arrival of the final calf that we have opened the barn door and bumbled in before we even notice that there's already a light inside.

The first thing I think is, *I didn't know the cows had flashlights.* And then, *How can a cow turn on a flashlight? Surely not with its hooves!*

Sometimes, it's easier to think silly things rather than face the dreadful truth.

The truth, of course, is that the flashlights belong to soldiers. Russian soldiers.

CHAPTER 19

There are seven Russian soldiers in the barn. We squint into the light of their flashlights.

I sweep Mia onto my hip and reach for Otto, but he has stepped *toward* the soldiers. I can see that he is dazed, baffled. He has come here to watch another miracle, another beautiful calf being born, but instead he has walked into a trap. He pulls off the pretty blue hat, scratches his head, and puffs out his cheeks.

One of the soldiers shouts something in Russian. Otto flinches but he doesn't run away.

I step forward to protect him, but another soldier steps between us and points a gun at me. My head swirls and my stomach lurches. I want to faint and vomit, both at the same time, but I have Mia in my arms, and I must keep her and Otto safe.

The soldiers are all shouting now, waving their guns and flashlights.

I see Otto's confusion and fear turn to anger. He squashes his hat in his hands. His shoulders hunch and his face screws up in readiness for the curses that are bubbling and boiling and rising to the surface.

'Oh no,' I moan.

'Hitler is a swine!' shouts Otto. One of the soldiers growls at him.

Otto reels around to face that soldier. 'Hitler is a swine!' he repeats. 'A big fat smelly swine. Hitler stole my papa and my mama and grandparents, and then he ran away like a coward with his curly little piggy tail between his legs and left us all alone to defend our country, but we can't because we are just children. And now, thanks to Hitler, the King of Swines, you dirty Russians are here in our barn, scaring our cows!'

The soldiers are stunned by this small boy—the redness of his face, the volume of his words, the rage that crackles around him like flak exploding in the sky. They tighten their circle around him and stare.

My stomach lurches again. I'm going to vomit.

Otto stamps his foot and bellows what might be his last words ever. 'I *hate* Hitler!'

I open my mouth to scream but nothing comes out.

The barn is silent. Deadly silent. Not even the cows make a sound.

And then, a soldier chuckles. With a heavy accent, he echoes Otto's words, 'I hate Hitler!' Then he says something about Hitler in Russian.

His comrades sling their guns over their shoulders and laugh. He has translated Otto's words and they like it!

'Otto,' I gasp, 'say more. Tell them more bad things about Hitler.'

It's only too easy for my little brother.

'Hitler is a goat,' he shouts, 'with fleas crawling all over his bottom!'

The Russian soldier translates and his comrades laugh. 'Hitler is a pile of poo in a chamber pot!' shouts Otto. Another translation and more laughter.

Then Otto pulls his trump card out of his pocket. He sits the squashed blue hat back on his head, puts his hands on his hips, lifts his chin, and sings the song he has been writing in his head and rehearsing all week.

'Hitler is a smelly swine.
He rolls in mud at half past nine.
At half past ten he does a poo,
Then eats it up at half past two.'

It's not fine poetry. The tune is not Beethoven. But the soldiers love it.

They stagger about, roaring with laughter, clutching at one another's sleeves. They get Otto to sing the song three more times, then they all begin to sing—in Russian, in German, in a strange mix of the two. They dance around the barn, cursing Hitler, dragging Otto in to join them.

When they've had enough, the soldier who translated Otto's curses turns to me and says, 'Now we will go into the house and you will please make us potato soup.'

Otto's naughtiness has saved us.

I don't know how to make Russian potato soup, but I don't tell the soldiers. I boil potatoes and mash them with lots of butter and salt, then add water until it's thin enough to slurp from a spoon.

While I'm cooking, Otto stokes the fire and runs back and forth taking tea to the soldiers.

The soldiers adore Mia. They take it in turns to bounce her upon their knees and teach her Russian nursery rhymes. Mia claps and sings in her garbled baby way and seems delighted with her new friends. But I am scared. These are Russians. Russians shoot papas who limp and boys like Jakob. Russians destroy villages and fire rockets at women and children and kind-hearted horses like Mozart. Tears run down my cheeks and fall into the pot of soup.

The soldiers crowd around the table and eat greedily— potato soup, the rest of our cheese, bread and butter, and all the preserved plums. Otto and I wait on them like servants.

Mia sits at the table with her own bowl of potato soup, eating it with her fingers and dribbling it down her chin. The soldiers cheer at everything she does, and Mia gurgles and grins like an angel. I am furious that these monsters are treating my little sister like a toy.

When their supper is eaten, one of the soldiers grabs Otto and stands him in the middle of the table. They want him to perform. He is their circus monkey, and it's time for him to dance and sing once more.

Otto stares at me, eyes filling with tears. He's scared and now, when he knows he has to, he can't curse.

'Just think of Papa and Mama,' I whisper, 'and how angry you are.' I can't believe that I'm encouraging him, but once again the rules have changed.

Otto nods. He clenches his fists, closes his eyes, and breathes deeply. His face turns red and—boom!—the fury arrives.

'Hitler is a worm!' he bellows, and stamps his foot so the bowls on the table rattle.

The soldier who speaks German repeats the words in Russian, and Otto bellows them again in the soldiers' own language. They laugh and bang their fists on the table.

Mia bangs her fists on the table too and shouts, 'Worm!'

The soldiers are off again, laughing, roaring, clutching their bellies.

The Wolf children are a huge success. I wonder how long it will last.

The soldiers sleep in the bedroom and on the soft chairs by the fire. Otto, Mia, and I sleep in the larder.

The German-speaking soldier gives us two eiderdowns and two pillows. He points to his chest and says, 'I am Dmitri.' It's a nice name and the bedding is a kind gesture, but it's not enough to stop me from hating him.

I clear the bottom shelves in the larder and make up two

beds—Otto and Mia on the bottom shelf, me on the next one up.

'That's not fair,' complains Otto. 'I want the top bunk.'

I can't describe how happy his words make me feel. They are so normal—just the sort of thing a seven-year-old boy should say. And exactly the way he should say it—high-pitched and whining.

I swap beds with Otto and curl up with Mia on the shelf where the cabbages and potatoes used to live.

'Mia love Lees,' murmurs Mia, and soon she is snoring.

'I wish I were a baby,' Otto grumbles. 'How can anyone sleep when the Russians are in the very next room?'

I start to sing a lullaby—one with stars and lambs and sheep.

'Mia's already asleep,' Otto mutters.

But I keep singing, and his breathing soon becomes slow and heavy.

I finish the lullaby, but I don't sleep.

CHAPTER 20

Early in the morning, Dmitri wakes me and beckons me out of my larder shelf, into the kitchen. I think he must want me to cook breakfast. But then he opens the door and points outside. I don't want to go outside. I don't want to leave Mia and Otto alone in the house. I don't want to be alone in the snow. I shake my head and refuse to move.

Dmitri grabs my hand and pulls me toward the door, but I won't go. He tugs a little harder. I scream and kick and bite his hand so hard that I taste blood in my mouth.

He lets go and yells in Russian.

When he turns to me once more, I flinch, expecting to be hit.

Instead he says, 'We are going to the cows.'

He uses his hands, not to hit, but to make a milking action, and I feel ashamed of myself. I have never milked a cow in my life, but I will try.

In the barn, the cows greet me with low moos and blinking lashes. One of the calves, Ginger, runs over and licks my fingers. Dmitri smiles and scratches Ginger behind her ears. I can see from the gentleness of his touch and the softening of his face that he likes animals.

Together, we find milking stools and buckets. I sit beside one of the cows. She doesn't mind that I am here, pressed up against her belly. It seems that she's been milked before.

'Thank you,' I whisper. 'I will try not to hurt you.'

I tug at her teat, but nothing happens. The cow turns her head and stares at me, her eyes wide. She seems to be saying, 'What *are* you doing, Liesl?' but she doesn't kick or walk away. She trusts me.

I hear the steady rhythm of squirting milk as Dmitri fills the bucket beneath his cow. I try again, but nothing comes out. I switch my hand to another teat, but the bucket remains dry.

I call to Dmitri, 'I think the calf has drunk everything.' He frowns. He doesn't understand.

I lift my bucket and show him the clean, dry bottom.

He chuckles, stands, and walks to my cow. Reaching past my hands, he grabs two of the teats and slowly, but firmly, rolls his fingers in a downward squeeze. A stream of milk squirts into the bucket.

Dmitri stands, then demonstrates the milking action again with one hand on the pointer finger of his other hand. He nods to indicate that I should try.

I reach for the cow's teats once more and do the rolling

squeeze. A small jet of milk falls into the bucket and I jump with surprise. I look up at Dmitri and smile.

He nods and smiles back at me and there, in that moment, I see my papa's eyes. Papa's eyes in a Russian soldier's face!

Confused, I turn back to the cow. I start milking, and after a few more successful squeezes, Dmitri returns to his own cow.

We milk a little from each of the cows, and I realize that Dmitri is being careful to leave plenty for the calves. I am annoyed and confused and relieved, for I can no longer deny it. This Russian soldier who is my enemy is a kind man.

The other soldiers are pigs. They drink all of the milk before Mia or Otto get a drop. Then they sit around the kitchen table, banging their fists until I have made more potato soup. What sort of animals have potato soup for breakfast?

When the soup is gone, they eat the rest of the preserved fruit, and I start to worry about how quickly the larder shelves are emptying. What will we eat when the Russians have gone? At least now I know how to milk the cows.

After breakfast, one of the soldiers stands, knocks his chair over, and stomps on it, breaking it apart. Then he picks up the pieces, walks across to the fire, and tosses them on. He has used his chair for firewood!

None of the other soldiers seem surprised or annoyed by his actions. They carry on chatting, laughing, passing Mia around from knee to knee.

Throughout the day, whenever the fire dies down, another chair is broken and burned.

I explain to Dmitri that there is a pile of dry wood at the back of the barn, enough to see them through to the summer, but he shrugs.

'They cannot be bothered. And we cannot carry the chairs with us when we go.'

I do not understand the way he thinks. I open my mouth to say that we are guests in this house, that the furniture belongs to a family just like mine, just like his. Nothing here should be burned or stolen. I also want to point out that if they burn all the chairs, there will be nothing left to sit on. It's so stupid. But no words come out.

Instead, I remember rockets exploding through ice, and wagons sinking, and dragging Otto across the frozen lagoon. And suddenly the chairs seem unimportant next to all the other dreadful things these Russian soldiers must have done since marching into East Prussia.

While I am standing there, lost for words, Mia toddles by and tosses a rolling pin into the fire. She turns toward us, dusts her hands like she has seen the soldiers do, and grins.

My baby sister is turning into a Russian monster!

Over the next two days, the Russians eat and sleep and slowly burn the house from the inside out. Chairs, chopping boards, drawers, picture frames, wardrobe doors, and shelves all become nothing more than fuel to keep us warm. Sheets and burlap sacks and straw brooms burn hot and fast. Blankets smoke and stink. A mantel clock provides steady, solid fuel until the wood casing is gone. Then the metal workings melt to a sad, wonky lump.

The soldiers grow bored with Otto's Hitler ditties, so he makes fun of the other leaders he knows.

'Winston Churchill has a face like a turnip!' he shouts. 'Franklin Roosevelt picks his nose and wipes it in his books!'

'Gustave Eiffel has rats nesting in his beard!'

Otto cannot remember the name of the French president, so he seizes on the next best thing—the creator of the Eiffel Tower.

I am worried because England, America, and France are *friends* of the Russians. But the soldiers don't mind. They are happy to mock anyone, as long as they are not Russian. They slap their legs and laugh and pass their cigarettes to Otto for him to try.

Otto puffs and coughs and runs to the kitchen sink and vomits. This pleases the soldiers even more. Their performing monkey never fails to come up with something new.

On the fourth evening, Dmitri and I are working together in the barn feeding the cows.

'My men have rested enough,' says Dmitri. 'Tomorrow we must go.'

Tomorrow! A smile tickles the corners of my mouth.

Tomorrow we will be rid of the Russians and the farm will be ours once more.

CHAPTER 21

'Up! Up!' Dmitri wakes us before the sun has risen. 'Dress in your warmest clothes. It will be a long day's march.'

Otto and I stare at Dmitri's back as he leaves the larder.

The Russians are taking us with them!

'Please, Dmitri,' I beg, running after him, 'let us stay.'

Dmitri's papa-eyes are soft and kind, but his words are not the ones I want to hear.

'The food is almost gone. Soon you will have nothing to eat. It is better this way. We will feed you. We will protect you.' He squeezes my shoulder. 'There will be more Russians coming through this way soon. Not all Russian soldiers are as kind and good as my men.'

I stare as two of the soldiers walk through the house, laughing and swiping everything off the shelves with the butts of their rifles. Glasses, plates, and jars smash across the kitchen floor. These are the *good* Russians.

I rescue our family photos from where they have fluttered down to the hearth of the open fireplace and shove them deep down into the pocket of my coat.

In the farmyard, four soldiers are herding the cows and calves out of the barn.

'You're taking the cows!' I gasp.

Dmitri nods. 'We will take them with us to the Red Army camp, and from there they will be sent east to Russia.'

'But the calves are so little. They'll get tired.'

'We will go slowly,' he says.

I stare past Dmitri, past the barn and into the forest we came through on the day we escaped the icy waters of the Vistula Lagoon. Mama might come through the forest one day soon, looking for us. But we won't be here.

'All will be good,' says Dmitri.

But there is nothing good about what is happening.

Otto also tries to keep us from being taken from the farm. We are all gathered outside, ready to leave, when he runs around kicking each of the soldiers in the shins. I understand what he's doing. He's hoping to annoy the Russians so much that they'll want to leave him behind. But it's dangerous. And it doesn't work.

One of the soldiers smacks Otto across the ear. It's not really hard enough to hurt, but it's a warning. Another soldier grabs Otto by the collar of his coat and drags him along for the first ten minutes of our march until he gets the message. We are going with the Russians whether we like it or not.

The day is icy cold but sunny. I think it might be March, because it feels like spring is trying to break free from the winter chill, but I no longer know the date. Just as I no longer know where I am in East Prussia.

The soldiers take it in turns to carry Mia. She babbles and sings as though she's out on a family picnic, then falls asleep and snores. The soldiers adore everything about her, and I'm glad to see that my baby sister has this magic power of dragging the kindness from deep within a Russian soldier's heart.

We walk through the forest and out into open fields, white with snow. We pass three farms, all burned to the ground. A fourth still stands, but the yard is filled with snow-covered mounds with odd things poking through—bed knobs, table legs, wardrobe doors. There's an eiderdown caught in the branches of a tree, a chair and a pretty red-and-white patch-work quilt in another. It's ridiculous, like something from pictures in a storybook.

Otto slips his hand into mine. 'Why do they do this, Liesl?'

'I don't know,' I whisper. 'All I know is that war does not make sense. The things that people do in a war are not the things they would do if they were at home with their fami-lies.'

'*We've* done things we wouldn't do if we were at home,' says Otto.

He pulls the collar of his coat aside to show the blue sweater he's stolen from the farmhouse. I do the same and show him my red sweater, and we giggle.

Even the giggling doesn't make sense, here, now, when we are being kidnapped by Russian soldiers.

Farther along the road, there's a field filled with trucks, jeeps, tanks—all blown apart or tipped upside down. Battle leftovers. The snow lies thickly around the vehicles, and I'm grateful, because I don't want to see what lies beneath.

We walk on and on, and my feet grow numb. The little calves grow tired, and one by one, the soldiers pick them up and carry them over their shoulders.

By midafternoon, everyone is weary. We enter a deserted village and Dmitri announces that we will stop for the night.

It's hard to find a building that hasn't had all the windows and doors torn off, but the schoolhouse on the edge of town is mostly whole. The soldiers carry the calves inside and the cows follow. Two of the soldiers search the village and return pushing a hand wagon full of straw, which they spread on the floor—dinner for the cows and beds for us.

We are back to sleeping like animals. At least Mia will be able to huddle with the calves and stay warm.

I wake feeling cold and sore. My eyes prickle with tears when I remember where we are. Or rather, when I remember that

I *don't* know where we are. Because if *I* don't know, Mama won't know.

I change Mia's diaper and throw the dirty one away. Hopefully we'll find more sheets or towels we can use at our next stop. Maybe soon Mia will learn to use a chamber pot. Dmitri milks one of the cows, just a little, and gives all the milk to Mia, Otto, and me. Two of the Russian soldiers frown at us as we drink, but I stare right back at them until they turn away.

How dare they make us feel bad for drinking milk? We are children. Mia is a baby. Everyone knows that children need milk for their teeth and bones. I hate Russians. I hate them so much.

Dmitri picks up Mia. She squeezes his nose and gurgles, 'Mia love Dimi!'

Dmitri's eyes soften and fill with tears. My breath catches. Dmitri passes Mia back to me and whispers, 'I miss my three daughters.' He walks outside and lights a cigarette and wanders away down the street on his own.

So I don't hate Dmitri.

But I hate *all* other Russians.

There is smoke in the distance. No cannon fire, but lots of thick black smoke, and we are walking straight toward it.

At the top of a small rise, we find ourselves looking down into a village that is all ablaze. The black skeletons of roofs and walls try to stand against the raging fire, but even as we watch, they sag and cave in and get gobbled up by the flames.

Trees on the edge of the village catch fire and pass the flames to a barn and three sheds. Everything is being consumed, except for the church steeple. It pokes up in the middle of the smoke and fire and charcoal, a proud German defying the Red Army. I love that steeple.

We keep walking, and as we reach the first smoldering ruins, we meet more Russian soldiers. They are warming their hands over a pile of coals that might once have been a henhouse or an outhouse or a garden shed. They chat with Dmitri and his men. They scowl at Mia, Otto, and me.

'There must have been a battle,' I say to Otto. 'I suppose the people in this village tried to fight against the Russians.'

'No,' says Dmitri. 'The people in this village ran away before these men arrived.' His face clouds over. 'They have burned the village because they thought it would be fun.'

I stare at the smoldering remains of houses, shops, a school, and, farther afield, farms, houses, and barns. 'Why?'

One of the Russians who has been warming his hands at the coals strides over to Otto, Mia, and me.

'Why not?' he replies in German. 'You Germans have been so rich. You had beautiful houses, larders full of food, barns full of animals, silos full of grain. In Russia, we had so little, barely enough to eat, and yet you Germans marched in and took everything. *You* have done bad things to Russia. Just for the fun of it. So now we are doing bad things to you.

Just for the fun of it. Just because we can. You dirty Germans deserve it.'

'That's not true,' I say.

The soldier spits at my feet.

Dmitri drags the soldier away, shouting at him in Russian.

Otto stares at me. '*We* didn't do bad things to Russia,' he whispers. 'We were at school, learning our times tables.'

I nod but don't say anything, because now I am wondering. *Have* the Germans done the same things as these horrible Russians are doing?

Otto tugs at my hand. 'I did kick a cat one time,' he confesses. 'His name was Ivan. Ivan is a *Russian* name, isn't it, Liesl?' His voice wobbles. 'I kicked a *Russian* cat. I shouldn't have done it, but he was teasing a poor little mouse and I wanted him to let it go.'

I want to tell the angry soldier that Germans are good people and that Adolf Hitler is a kind and loving leader. We are not like the horrible, nasty Russians. We are not!

'I hate beetroot soup,' Otto continues, now clutching his face with both hands. 'Beetroot soup is Russian, isn't it, Liesl? Maybe the soldier means I've been a bad boy because I said rude things about Russian food . . . about *his* food.'

Are the Germans like the Russians? My eyes fill with tears.

'I'm sorry, Liesl,' whimpers Otto. 'Please don't cry. I promise I'll be a good boy from now on. I will never kick a

Russian cat again, and I'll only say good things about Russian food. I won't even kick the Russian soldiers in the shins. I promise, Liesl. I'll be good. I'll be *really* good! Just don't cry.'

But I can't help it. My eyes overflow and tears stream down my face. Because now I am truly worried.

Are the Germans *worse* than the Russians?

CHAPTER 22

We are on a farm. It's not like the farm where the calves were born. This is a grand farm that has a manor house with white walls and a red-tiled roof, and lots of extra buildings— stables, barns, sheds, a smokehouse, and workers' cottages. Everywhere there are Russian soldiers, Russian tanks, Russian trucks, and those big clusters of Russian cannons called Stalin's organs. The Russians have taken this beautiful East Prussian farm and turned it into an ugly Red Army camp.

We came here by truck, and I'm not sure where we are, except that we are closer to Lithuania. Maybe we are closer to home, too, but the soldiers laughed when I asked. They made exploding actions with their hands, and one waved his arms in the air and screamed like a child, and I felt sick so I didn't ask any more questions.

Dmitri has found us a room in the attic of the manor

house. His room is next door. It looks like he stays close so we won't escape, but I know it's so he can keep us safe. Russian soldiers come in all shapes and sizes and ages, but most of them are mean. And they hate Germans. All Germans. Even children like Otto and Mia and me. They don't even call us by our names. They call us German Girl, German Boy, and German Baby.

I lie awake at night, pressing the family photos to my chest, repeating our proper names. Is this why Opa made Otto and me recite all the family names that last morning before we said goodbye? Because he wanted us to remember that we are Wolfs? That we matter? Did he know the Russians would try to tell us that we are nothing more than dirty little Germans who deserve whatever they do to us?

I lie awake at night wondering. Wondering if this is true. I think the *Russians* are dirty. And smelly. And I don't like them. Except for Dmitri because of his papa-eyes and the way he is kind to the cows.

We've been here for two weeks, and I've been forced to work in the kitchen, peeling potatoes. So many potatoes! I have blisters and cuts all over my hands. But at least the cooks are not soldiers—not the type who carry guns and wear helmets. And Viktor, the baker, is kind. He's more interested in making bread than being mean. I suppose I like Viktor, too.

Mia stays at my side, playing with spoons and bowls, sucking on lumps of bread and rubbing flour into her hair. The cooks call her their little *kroshka*. I think it means 'darling' or 'angel.' I know it's a good word, something that means they adore her, because they say it with singsong voices and soft eyes, and it makes Mia smile.

Mia always brings joy. She is treasure. For me. For Otto. For anyone she meets.

Otto is made to work in the stable and the barn. I am cross that the Russians are treating us like slaves, but Otto likes being with the animals, especially Dog the calf.

Viktor passes me a loaf of bread. It looks like a black brick and feels just as heavy, but it's warm and smells delicious.

'Here,' he says. 'Go and see your brother. Have a rest. Take a picnic in the sunshine.'

I thank Viktor, tuck the bread under my arm, and hoist Mia onto my back. I am too tired from all the potato peeling to carry her on my hip, so now we do piggybacks when we want to get somewhere quickly.

The sun is *not* shining outside, no matter what Viktor says. The sky is filled with clouds and there's a chill in the air. It will be freezing again tonight, even though it's supposed to be spring.

I dash across the farmyard before any soldiers can yell at me or steal my bread. I duck into the stables and find Otto sitting on a bale of hay, talking to a Russian soldier. They are chattering away in a jumble of German as though they are old friends, and I feel a stab of anger that Otto is being so kind to the enemy.

'Hello!' The soldier stands. 'I am Alexi, and I am very pleased to meet you.'

Alexi smiles and his brown eyes sparkle. He is very young. He reminds me of Jakob, the boy soldier who went off to war with Papa, the boy soldier who went missing in action with Papa. My breath catches, and suddenly I feel sorry for Alexi.

I nod, and even smile a little. 'Hello. Your German is good. I'm Liesl. And this little bear on my back is Mia.'

'Ullo! Ullo!' sings Mia as I plop her down beside Otto.

She opens and closes her chubby little fingers in a wave. 'My sisters,' says Otto.

Alexi pulls a photo from his pocket and passes it to me. '*My* sisters,' he says.

There is a big family standing outside a small house—a square mother with a scarf on her head, a thin father with a fur hat, Alexi in a shirt and pants held up with suspenders, and lots of girls.

I count them and shout, '*Seven* sisters!'

Alexi rolls his eyes.

I smile and pass the photo to Otto. He tilts it to the left and to the right, and frowns. He holds it up close to his nose, then yells, 'Your fly's unbuttoned, Alexi!'

Alexi snatches the photo and stares at it. He begins to laugh, softly at first, then louder and louder until he snorts. 'I did not notice it before!' He blushes and tucks the picture inside his coat. 'I will not show the picture to *anyone* ever again!' He shakes his head, slaps his forehead, and laughs some more.

And just like that, Alexi has become our friend.

Dmitri. Viktor. Alexi. That's *three* Russian friends. Astonishing.

It is bedtime, and when I go to change Mia's diaper, she is still dry.

She smiles at me and says, 'Mia want tinkle.'

I'm very excited that she's told me this. I knock on Dmitri's door. 'We need to use the bathroom. Mia needs to tinkle.'

Dmitri smiles and chucks Mia under the chin, his eyes as full of pride as though she were his own daughter. He understands how special this moment is.

He pulls on his coat and leads the way. He won't let us wander about alone.

We walk down the stairs and along the corridor, but the bathroom is already crowded with three Russian soldiers. They are peering into the toilet, muttering and rubbing their jaws.

Dmitri shouts at them and they step aside. He looks in the toilet and bursts out laughing. He beckons to Otto, Mia, and me. We, too, look in the toilet and burst out laughing. There is a pair of khaki socks floating in the water!

Dmitri chats with the men, then turns to us and explains. 'These men are peasants, simple farmers. They have never seen a flushing toilet. They think it is a place to wash their clothes.'

The men mutter and nod and argue with one another. They look like they're trying to solve a puzzle. Suddenly one notices the chain hanging from the tank above the toilet.

'Aha!' he cries and, before we can stop him, he reaches up and pulls it.

The toilet flushes and his socks disappear.

Otto and I laugh, but the Russian yells—at his friends, at Dmitri, at the now-empty toilet bowl.

Dmitri chuckles. 'He is calling the toilet a stealing machine.'

'A stealing machine!' repeats Otto. He smiles and nods at the soldier. 'That's a good name for a toilet. It's just that the things you want it to steal are tinkles and poos and toilet paper, not socks.'

Dmitri tries to explain to the soldiers what the toilet is *really* for, but they cannot believe it. Their faces fill with horror at the idea of pooing in this beautiful porcelain bowl, and they wander away, shaking their heads, casting looks of disgust back over their shoulders at Dmitri. Which makes me wonder: If they don't use the toilet for their business, where do they go?

Dmitri and Otto wait outside, and Mia does her first tinkle in a real toilet. Her eyes widen as she hears the tinkling sound, then she claps her hands.

I clap too. I am filled with pride. I smile and laugh.

I think, *This moment is treasure. Treasure to store up in my heart.*

And then I laugh some more, because who would think that a tinkle could be a treasure?

Viktor bakes a cake. A big fat Russian cake.

'It is called *medovik*,' he announces. 'Lots and lots of layers of cake made with honey, all joined together with sour cream.' He leans forward and lowers his voice. 'I used the honey that is supposed to be saved for Major Fedorov. I will probably be court-martialed and sent to Siberia, but at least I will go with a belly full of cake.'

The medovik is a celebration cake. Mia has been running around the kitchen all day singing, 'Mia tinkle toilet.' She is very proud of her latest achievement. So proud that she forgets to tell me when she needs to go again and tinkles all over the kitchen floor.

Viktor doesn't mind. He passes me the mop and bakes the medovik to celebrate Mia's big moment—the one in the toilet, not the one on the floor.

We sit around the large kitchen table. Mia is perched on a crate on top of a chair at the head of the table, clapping her hands.

Viktor cuts huge slices of medovik and passes them to Mia, me, and the three cooks. We eat in silence, the sweet honey layers melting in our mouths. Mia likes it so much that she doesn't even save any to rub in her hair.

Cake. It's like a birthday party. 'Viktor,' I gasp, 'what day is it today?'

'It is Friday,' he says.

'But what is the date?' I ask.

'The thirtieth of March.'

We have missed Mia's birthday. Her second birthday. 'Mia turned two three weeks ago,' I announce.

Viktor and the other cooks clap and cheer and sing a song in Russian. Then we eat a second piece of cake to celebrate.

When Mia is finished, she shouts, 'Mia love cake yummy!'

It is the longest sentence she has ever said, and we celebrate by eating yet another piece of cake.

Except for Mia. This piece she rubs into her hair.

CHAPTER 23

Alexi stands at the door to our room. It's late at night and he is filthy and smelly and I think the dark smear across his cheek is blood. I know he's been out fighting all day, even though he doesn't say so. Fighting against Germans. Fighting against people like Papa and Jakob. For a moment I hate Alexi like I hate the other Russian soldiers. But then I see the Jakob bits in his face, the bits that remind me that he is just a big boy, and I see how stupid I am being. Alexi can't help being a Russian soldier any more than I can help being a German kitchen slave.

Dmitri bursts out of his room, scowling, ready to yell, ready to keep us safe. But then he sees Alexi, and his shoulders soften and his mouth widens into a smile. 'Alexi! My boy!' They hug and we can see that they are old friends.

They talk in Russian for a few minutes, then Alexi turns

to Otto and me and says, 'I have a gift for you.' He pulls a small wooden figure from his coat pocket. It's an old woman, wrinkled and stooped, her body following the twisted lines of the wood. 'I rescued it from a house . . . before the other soldiers burned it down.'

He blushes as though ashamed of his fellow soldiers, as though there is more to the story than burning down a house. I don't want to know, so I step forward and take the gift from his hand.

'Thank you,' I whisper.

Otto snatches the old woman from me and holds her up to the light. 'She's just like the witches in our bedtime stories, Liesl!' He turns to Dmitri and Alexi. 'Every night, our mama used to tell us stories about wicked witches and ferocious bears and horrible Russian soldiers and—' Otto stops and blushes. 'Sorry.'

Alexi shrugs. 'It is fine. I used to tell my little sisters bedtime stories about wicked witches and ferocious bears and horrible *German* soldiers, so I suppose we are even.'

Otto smiles.

'But sometimes,' Alexi goes on, 'instead of the stories, I played checkers with my little sisters.'

'Checkers!' cries Otto. 'I love checkers!'

'Me too,' says Alexi. 'It's my favorite game.'

'We could play checkers *together*,' says Otto. 'There are no Russian soldiers or German soldiers in a game of checkers.'

'Especially not in an *imaginary* game of checkers,' I say. I hold my hands out to show how empty they are. No board. No checkers. No game.

Alexi and Otto both slump their shoulders at the same time.

'Wait!' shouts Dmitri. He disappears back into his own room and returns with a ragged deck of cards. 'I will teach you a card game. It is called Durak.'

'Durak,' repeats Otto.

'Durak!' cheers Alexi.

We sit on the bed and Dmitri bosses us like a papa until we learn the rules, and then we give it a try. It is tricky and fun and we play it over and over again. Otto wins, then Alexi, then me, then Alexi again, then Dmitri, and we keep going until we have all lost and won so many times that we lose count and don't know who the victor is.

We play on and on, late into the night, laughing, shouting, throwing cards into the air, arguing, hugging, and creating a new kind of bedtime where there are no Russians or Germans, no soldiers or servants, no winners or losers, just friends and family.

And friends who feel strangely like family. And, most surprising of all, happiness.

Otto, Mia, and I are in the barn with the cows and the calves. Dog, Ginger, Wobbles, and Moo are growing big and rough, but they still love to be cuddled.

Mia kisses their slimy noses, and they lick her face until she squeals. 'Woof! Woof!'

Mia is speaking well but still gets confused about animal names and sounds. She insists that horses say 'quack' and hens say 'la-la.' And this week Dog has been a dog, a sheep, and a truck.

Otto moves a bale of hay and pulls out a wooden clipboard and a pencil. 'Ta-da!'

'Where did you get it?' I ask.

'I stole it,' he says, 'from one of the trucks, while the soldier was having a wee against the back tire.'

I nod. It's all right to steal from the Russians. Especially the ones that call us dirty Germans and wee against truck tires. They are our enemy.

Besides, the clipboard is for a good cause. We're going to make a game of checkers for Alexi and Dmitri. It's a surprise, a thank-you for being kind. Even though they are Russian. Even though we are German.

CHAPTER 24

Viktor and I stare out the kitchen window. The farmyard is full of soldiers, but today they are not marching out with their guns and helmets. Today, they are stumbling in with their arms full. They are carrying eiderdowns and feather pillows, fur coats and suitcases, piles of timber, glass panes from windows, trays piled high with knives and forks and teapots and gravy jugs, giant legs of ham, and crates stuffed with canned food. One soldier staggers into the farmyard with a double mattress balancing on his head!

'What are they doing?' I ask.

'They are going to send those things home,' says Viktor, 'to their families in Russia.'

'But those things do not belong to them,' I say.

Viktor shrugs. 'They do now.'

'They're taking so much!' I gasp.

'This is nothing,' grumbles Viktor. 'All over East Prussia they are pulling up railway tracks, dismantling factories, breaking down farm machinery, sending it all back to Russia.'

I open my mouth to protest, but then I remember what the soldier in the burning village said about the Germans stealing from the Russians. I close my mouth again.

Besides, Otto and I are making a game of checkers using a stolen clipboard and a stolen pencil, and I am wearing a stolen red sweater, stolen trousers, and stolen long johns. War turns everyone into thieves.

When my last potato is peeled, Viktor shoves another brick of bread into my hands and tells me to go and feed my brother.

I am scared to cross the farmyard when there are so many Russian soldiers about. I stay close to the buildings, Mia hanging from my back like a monkey, and keep moving. The Russians are busy with their stolen treasures and don't seem to notice that the dirty German children are in their midst.

I hitch Mia higher onto my back and make a dash toward the barn. I am halfway there when something slams into my body and knocks me to the ground. I lie in the melting snow, wrapped around my crying sister, trying to protect her from the second blow. But it doesn't come.

When I open my eyes, there's no one with raised fists or boots ready to kick. Instead, there's a Russian soldier sprawled on the ground beside me, dazed, a bicycle at his side.

I stare at the bicycle, and my heart is filled with memories.

Sunny summertime memories.

Otto and I are riding our bicycles up and down the cobbled street in front of our house, teeth and laughter rattling. We are riding along the country lanes, through clouds of butterflies, sticking our feet out past the pedals so we can feel the dandelions and wild oats whipping our legs. We are flying, giggling, screaming, racing dogs and birds and all the other children on their bikes.

But that was so very long ago. Before rubber was a luxury and flat tires could no longer be fixed but had to be cut up and nailed to the soles of our worn-out boots. Before our bikes were taken to the school for Scrap Metal Day so they could be melted down and turned into tanks and airplanes and bombs that would help Germany win the war.

I lie on the ground, the damp soaking through my clothes, staring at the bicycle. Its pale-green paint is chipped, and it has rope instead of rubber for tires, but it is all in one piece, and it is beautiful.

Alexi hovers over me. He lifts Mia into his arms and kisses away her tears. 'Liesl,' he shouts, 'are you all right? Are you hurt?'

I stand up and smile. I step over the soldier, who is rubbing his forehead, and lift up the bike. I put one foot on the pedal, push off with the other, and I ride. Slowly at first, because it's been a long time since I have done it.

I weave in and out of the soldiers and the piles of pillows and the wooden crates full of food. My body grows straighter, my legs stronger, as they remember how this works. I pedal harder and harder. My hair flies out behind me, flapping in the wind, and now I am going so fast that I think I could overtake a dog, a bird, even an airplane.

I complete a full circuit of the farmyard and ride back to the soldier. I give him his bicycle and thank him in Russian. But before I can turn away, three more Russians with bicycles have joined us, and they are all yelling and poking at me.

Alexi laughs. 'They do not know how to ride their new bicycles,' he explains. 'They have ridden horses and even cows, but never a bicycle. Most of these soldiers had never even laid eyes on a bicycle before they marched into East Prussia.'

'Then why did they steal them?' I ask.

Alexi shrugs. 'Because they look special. Because they could.'

The Russians point and shout again.

'And now they want *you* to teach them to ride,' says Alexi.

I spend the rest of the day teaching Russian soldiers to ride bicycles. The ones who don't ride watch and laugh and cheer. Alexi holds Mia on his shoulders, and she claps and cheers too. It is better than a trip to the circus.

I start with the soldier who knocked Mia and me to the ground. I think it will be good if he learns how to ride properly before he hurts anyone else. I hold the back of his bicycle seat and run along behind him, shouting words of encouragement that he doesn't understand. When I let go, he looks around and sees that I am no longer there and rides into the wall of the barn. He staggers to his feet, kicks the bicycle, and storms away.

Another soldier rushes forward to claim the bicycle. He tells me his name is Igor and he smiles. I smile back, grateful for this small show of kindness.

This time I start by demonstrating how I ride, then hand the bicycle over to Igor. He is tall and thin like an athlete and learns quickly. I run along behind the bike, holding on to the seat, but he is sure and steady and barely needs my help. He keeps the wheels straight and doesn't wobble once. He pedals faster and faster until I can no longer keep up and have to let go. Igor rides on across the farmyard, yelling.

I think it is pride, celebration, but Alexi runs to my side, laughing so hard that he staggers about, Mia tottering on his shoulders. 'He is shouting that you have not shown him how to stop.'

I watch, eyes wide, as Igor zooms out of the farmyard, along the driveway, into the road, then disappears over the crest of the hill.

Now I give a lesson to three soldiers all together. I start by showing them how I pedal forward to go, and backward to stop. They laugh and nod and point into the distance, to where Igor has gone. I grimace and they laugh some more.

I soon have them all riding around the farmyard, starting, stopping, weaving in and out of jeeps and crates. They laugh and call out, 'Liesl! Liesl!' wanting me to see how clever they are. They are like little children who need always to be the center of attention. Little children buried inside the bodies of mean Russian soldiers.

Last of all, I teach Captain Sokolov to ride. He is a giant of a man and his bike is tiny—made for a child. He looks like a performing bear riding a tricycle, but he is nimble and swift and joins his men in a game of tag around and around the farmyard. Then he passes his bicycle to me, and I join the fun. I zip in and out of the Russian cyclists, making them wobble and roar in fear.

Otto finishes his work in the barn and joins us. One of the soldiers lifts him onto his handlebars and zooms around. Otto laughs and his blond hair flaps about his head. He looks happy, just like he did in the days when we rode our own bikes along the country lanes.

'Look! Look!' Alexi has passed Mia to Captain Sokolov and is standing on a rock wall, pointing into the distance.

We all stop riding and watch as Igor cycles down the driveway and back into the farmyard. He tries to slow down by dragging his boots along the ground but does not stop until he crashes into a tank. When he gets to his feet, I notice that his face is scratched and his uniform is torn. He shouts and waves his arms about, and his fellow soldiers laugh.

Alexi says, 'He rode for many miles. He says he may have reached Lithuania if he hadn't hit a bump and run into a blackberry bush.'

I scrunch my nose and try to remember the Russian words Alexi has taught me that mean 'sorry.' But nothing comes out except a giggle. I clamp my hand over my mouth. Igor steps forward. I think he's going to yell at me. But instead he reaches into his pocket and pulls something out. It's a daffodil—the first flower I have seen this year. It is a sign that spring has truly arrived. It is a reminder that there are still beautiful things to be found in the world. And it is a gift, from one friend to another. I take the daffodil and smile.

This has been a good day. But confusing.

For I think I am starting to like the Russians.

CHAPTER 25

Captain Sokolov, the gentle bear on the tricycle, has been so very kind these last three weeks. He slips into the kitchen when he has time and bounces Mia upon his knee. He sings her Russian nursery rhymes, tells her Russian fairy tales about a witch called Baba Yaga and a beautiful girl called Vasilisa, and kisses her golden curls when she uses Russian words. He brings her gifts—a doll, a tiny wooden train, a little china teapot. I know they are stolen from German homes after the families have fled. Stolen toys that once belonged to other German children like Mia. But Mia is happy, and I am glad that she has something to play with.

'Mia is a princess!' says Captain Sokolov every time he hands her back to Viktor or me. He says it in Russian, but I am learning more and more of this strange language every day.

But today, Captain Sokolov sits Mia on the floor and says

something else. I think I understand the Russian words, but when he's gone, I check with Viktor.

'Did he say that his wife would like a little girl like Mia?'

Viktor sighs. 'Yes.' He wipes his hand across his forehead, leaving a streak of flour. 'Although he might have said "love," not "like" . . . and perhaps it was "will," not "would."'

I frown as I try to piece the new words together. And then my neck prickles.

It is early morning, still dark, when Alexi bursts into our room.

'Quickly!' he shouts. 'Put on all your clothes. *Everything!*' We do as we are told. We don't ask why. Dress first. Get ready to flee. Ask questions later. It's the safest way to go about it. We have learned a lot in the last few months.

While we are dressing, Alexi wakes Dmitri and drags him into our room. 'We must help them run away,' he says.

'Don't be stupid!' Dmitri snaps. 'They are children. They will be all alone. It is too foolish. Too dangerous. Much better that they stay here with us.'

Alexi grabs Dmitri by the shoulders and hisses into his face. 'It is not safe here! Captain Sokolov is leaving, and he wants to take Mia with him. As a gift for his wife.'

I freeze, halfway through buttoning Mia's cardigan. 'But Captain Sokolov is our *friend*!'

I stare at Alexi, willing him to agree. I want him to smile and say that of course Captain Sokolov is our friend. He would not do anything to harm me or Otto or Mia. But Alexi says nothing. His eyes shift away from mine.

Suddenly, I hate Captain Sokolov. Yesterday he was my friend, but today I hate him. He was pretending to be a gentle bear with a kind heart, but really he is a big bad wolf. I hate Captain Sokolov! I hate him!

I sweep Mia into my arms and squeeze her so tightly that she squirms and whines, 'No, no!'

But I hold fast, as though I can keep her with me just by the strength of my arms. I know it's stupid. As if I could win a battle against Captain Sokolov and his Red Army soldiers.

Dmitri slumps onto the bed. 'Captain Sokolov probably thinks he is doing a good thing—giving Mia a mama, his wife a daughter.' He rubs the back of his neck.

I can see that he is wondering which is worse: for Otto, Mia, and me to be alone without food, shelter, or anyone to protect us; or for Mia to be taken away.

'I promised Mama,' I whisper. 'I promised I would look after Mia and Otto. I cannot do that unless we are all together.'

Otto runs to my side and wraps his arms around Mia and me. 'Mama wants us to stay together so she can find us all at the same time,' he says.

'Please!' I beg Dmitri. 'You would like to find *your* three daughters all together when you get home from the war, wouldn't you?'

Dmitri nods. 'Yes. Yes. You are right.' He springs to his feet, rips the blankets from our bed, and makes them into a bundle that Otto can carry over his shoulder.

We put our old coats over the top of our stolen clothes and pull our woolen hats down over our heads. Alexi pops a box of matches into Otto's pocket.

I check that the family photos are still in my pocket, then hoist Mia onto my back.

I spot the corner of the wooden clipboard poking out from beneath my pillow. 'The checkers,' I murmur. 'We haven't even played yet.'

Otto grabs our homemade board with the squares drawn on in pencil, and the tin containing twenty pebbles and twenty dried beans. He hands them to Alexi.

'Your own special game of checkers,' says Otto. 'You will have to practice with Dmitri, and when the war is over, I will challenge you to a game.'

Such a beautiful idea. But it feels a bit like another story. Like when Opa said he and Oma would rest in the church and catch up to us later.

Alexi nods and tucks the clipboard inside his jacket, the tin in his pocket. Then he and Dmitri sneak us down the stairs, out of the house, across the dark yard, and into the smokehouse.

Alexi picks up a sack hidden in the corner and thrusts it into my hand. 'Bread, smoked sausage, and cheese. From Viktor.' He sniffs.

Is he smelling the sausage, or is he crying?

I turn to Dmitri and ask, 'Where will we go?'

'Just away,' he says. 'Find shelter where you can, but try to keep clear of the Russians.' He grimaces. 'Russians are bad news.'

'You aren't,' I whisper.

Dmitri nods. 'And you three are not so bad for Germans.' He steps forward and wraps his arms around us. Alexi wraps his arms from the other side. We are a Dmitri-Liesl-Otto-Mia-Alexi blob, and it feels like family.

'I wish Mama and Papa were here,' Otto sobs.

'I wish my daughters were here,' says Dmitri.

'I wish the war was over and we were all at home,' whispers Alexi.

We are all the same deep down. German. Russian. Children. Soldiers.

Alexi gives us a final squeeze, then he walks outside without looking back.

Dmitri says, 'You are strong, Liesl. You can do this.' But I don't even know what *this* is!

Dmitri kisses us each on the forehead and follows Alexi outside.

Soon, we hear an argument from somewhere in the farmyard. It is Dmitri shouting at Alexi. Glass shatters and there is more shouting, and I realize they are creating a diversion.

I hitch Mia a little higher on my back, take Otto by the hand, and run. Away from the farm that has been turned into a Red Army camp, across the muddy meadow, over the hill, and into the forest. We do not stop until dawn breaks and we can see nothing around us but trees.

I let Mia slip to the ground, and I double over, hands on knees, gasping for breath.

Otto is gulping in air and cursing Hitler and ranting against the entire Red Army.

Mia has just wet her pants. And I am crying.

We have left without kissing Dog the calf goodbye. Without thanking Viktor for all his heavy black bread and light kindness. Without remembering the happy bits with stealing machines and bicycles and daffodils and honey-cake celebrations. Without Dmitri and Alexi.

We're free at last, and yet it feels like we have lost. Again.

WILD
WOLVES

CHAPTER 26

I wake to sunshine and the sound of a bird chirping. I keep my eyes closed and roll over onto my side. Something tickles my face. A feather from my eiderdown? I try to sweep the feather aside, but it's soft and cold and slimy and sticks to my cheek.

I scream and sit up. It's not a feather from my eiderdown because I am sleeping beneath a tree in a bed of scratchy blankets and leaves and moss. I scream some more and shake my hands.

Otto wakes and springs to his feet. 'Liesl!' he shouts. 'What is it?'

He gapes at me, then bursts out laughing. He pulls the slimy thing from my face and holds it out for me to see.

'A slug!' I cry.

'A slug,' says Otto.

Mia sits up, her hair tangled, her eyes droopy. But she doesn't speak.

Otto and I stare at each other, then stare at the slug.

Otto licks his lips and tilts his head to one side, a question in his eyes.

I look at him. 'Otto, don't,' I say. Who knows what disease a dirty slug might carry?

Otto doesn't care. He pops the slug into his mouth. He cringes at the first taste, chews with his mouth puckered, then swallows.

'Urgh!' I press my hands to my face. I'm disgusted. And I'm scared. . . . What if it makes him sick? But I'm starving too, so I peep through my fingers and ask, 'What's it like?'

'Slippery. Slimy. And a lot chewier than I expected.'

'And the flavor?'

'Delicious,' he lies. 'Tastes like the roast goose Mama cooked at Christmastime. But without the almond stuffing.'

Roast goose! My mouth waters, and suddenly I don't care about the danger. I just want to eat.

I *need* to eat.

We all do. I shrug. We pull the blankets back and crawl around, lifting leaves and bits of moss and sticks, until we each have a handful of slugs.

I offer one to Mia, but she pulls away.

I pop the slug into my mouth and shudder. I don't know which is worse—the slippery-sludgy sliminess, the bitter taste, the danger, or the thought that there's a live creature sliding across my tongue. I spit it out into my hand.

Otto snorts. 'You're a coward, Liesl!' He slurps a slug from his hand, chews, swallows, and rubs his tummy. 'Yum yum! Tastes like bratwurst!' He gobbles another and groans in delight. 'Mmmmmm! Tastes like marzipan!'

I take a deep breath, pop another slug in my mouth, and swallow it whole. It's the most disgusting thing I have done in my life, but I smile, rub my tummy, and sing, 'Deeeee-licious! Tastes like Black Forest cake!'

And so we eat our way through the slugs, pretending they are chocolate-coated cherries, bits of smoked sausage, meatballs, cinnamon biscuits, gingerbread men, anything but dirty slugs plucked from the forest floor.

I offer another to Mia. She picks it up between her fingers, then drops it. She whimpers and bursts into tears. I pull her into my lap, wrap her in my arms, and rock her back and forth while Otto eats the rest of the slugs.

We have been hiding in the forest for over a week now. Our food was all gone after three days. We ate nothing for two days, then Otto caught a frog. We stared at it for hours, and then we ate it. I cried, but Otto closed his eyes and pretended it was jelly. Mia refused to eat.

We've tried wild herbs, and grass that we *pretended* was wild herbs, and now slugs. Otto and I could probably survive for weeks on this horrible forest food, but Mia can't. She hasn't eaten since we finished the bread, and she's growing pale and thin and listless. Even now she has run out of energy to cry and is resting against my chest, sucking her thumb.

'We have to find food,' I tell Otto. 'Real food. For Mia.'

'But what about the Russians?' he asks. 'Dmitri said they are everywhere. Mean Russians.'

'We'll have to be careful. We'll sneak into an abandoned house, find food, then disappear back into the forest. No hanging around. No sleeping in beds or barns. Just grab and run.'

'Like thieves,' says Otto.

I blush. 'Yes.'

'I can do that!' he cries. 'I've done it before. Remember the clipboard and the pencil?'

I nod and give him my biggest smile. It's a smile of encouragement and shame. Because my little brother is a slug-eating thief and he's proud of it. Because I too am a slug-eating thief.

Otto and I take it in turns to piggyback Mia through the forest. I break twigs and kick patches of leaf litter aside as we go, making a kind of trail so we can find our way back to our coats and blankets.

We stop at a small brook and drink.

'Can we steal some boots?' asks Otto. 'Mine are rubbing. I think my feet have grown.'

I shrug. 'I suppose so. If we're going to steal food, I don't see what difference a pair of boots will make.'

'What about socks?' asks Otto. 'Can we steal them, too?'

I slurp some water from my cupped hand while I think about it. 'Yes. Boots and socks are what I'd call essentials. It's not wrong if we're taking things to survive.'

'What about chocolate, then?' asks Otto. 'Is that essential, or is it just for fun?'

'Mia love chocolate!' Mia claps her hands and smiles for the first time in days.

'Chocolate is essential!' I cry. 'It makes Mia happy. *And* it's food. Anything we can eat is essential.'

We peep out from the bushes at the edge of the forest. There is a farm nearby, but no signs of life—no smoke coming from the chimney, no animals in the yard, no laundry on the line.

We dash from tree to tree, making our way across a field, until we're close enough to see broken windows, a door hanging from just one hinge, and a wardrobe lying on its side in the front garden.

'The Russians have already been here,' says Otto.

'That doesn't mean they won't return!' I snap. 'Get ready to run! In and out! As fast as we can! Got it?'

Otto stares at me, his mouth open.

I realize how bossy I've been. I sound like a Red Army officer, not a well-behaved German girl.

'Sorry,' I say.

Otto shrugs. 'It's good advice.'

'Mia want chocolate,' my baby sister whispers into my ear, and she squeezes her hands more tightly around my neck.

'Me too,' I reply. 'Let's go.'

We run to the house and slip through the front door. Inside it stinks of rotten food and damp rugs. Everything has been swept from the shelves onto the floor, smashed, trampled, muddied.

I let Mia slide from my back. 'Don't touch anything,' I tell her. 'Yucky poo-poos.'

'Poo-poos,' says Mia, frowning.

My heart melts. She's so cute, even when she is dirty and thin and tired.

We wander upstairs, into the bedroom. A pigeon flaps around the ceiling.

'Shoo! Shoo!' Mia shouts, waving her arms in the air. The pigeon flies past us, its wings brushing my head, and slams into the one window that hasn't been broken. Stunned, it falls to the floor.

'Poor little thing!' I cry, scooping it up in my hands.

I take it to an open window and let it go.

'What did you do that for?' shouts Otto.

I stare at him. 'I was being *kind*.'

'Pigeons are food!' he shouts. 'They're like chicken and turkey and roast goose! Mia *loves* roast goose.'

My shoulders slump. 'I'm sorry, Otto,' I whisper. 'I'm sorry, Mia.'

I feel stupid, but I'm also glad. To eat a pigeon, you must first kill it. I'm not sure I could do such a thing. I'm still getting used to eating slugs.

There is nothing useful left in the bedroom, just torn pillows and scattered horsehair stuffing, so we head back downstairs.

There's a large mirror on the parlor wall. It's cracked and

has something smeared across the surface, but there's still enough mirror to give me a shock.

Inside the frame stand three dirty, ragged children. I recognize Otto and Mia because I look at them every day, but the tallest child, the girl, is not at all familiar. She's thin, with greasy, lank hair, and she's dressed like a boy. But the strangest thing about her is her eyes. They are too big, too watchful, too hard. They look like they've been stolen from an adult's face.

I step closer to the mirror. I lean forward and touch the girl. It's me, but it is not me.

'Liesl!' Otto tugs at my sweater. 'In and out, remember?'

We step over crumpled books and slashed cushions to the kitchen.

Otto whines, 'All the food has been eaten or stolen or trampled beneath big fat ugly Russian boots.'

My tummy rumbles and Otto's tummy replies.

Mia picks up something that might be an old sausage or a giant slug or a pair of moldy socks. She moves it toward her mouth, and I shout, 'No, Mia!' She drops it to the floor and begins to cry.

I scoop her up and march out into the yard. I look around. 'There must be *something* to eat!' I moan.

And then my eyes fall on the field on the far side of the barn. It's mostly bare, but I can see a few brown lumps scattered here and there.

'Potatoes!' I shout. 'Potatoes that have been missed during the harvest!'

'Tatoes!' shouts Mia, jiggling up and down in my arms as I run to the field.

I dig up a potato and wipe off as much dirt as I can before Mia snatches it from my hands. She grins and chomps down. She spits out the dirt and scrunches her nose at the raw, crunchy vegetable, but then she smiles. 'Mia love tatoes.' And she chomps on.

My heart leaps for joy. At last, something Mia can eat.

We dig up so many potatoes that we cannot carry them all in our pockets and hands. Otto runs to the barn and returns with an old wooden wheelbarrow. We toss our potatoes into it and return to the house. I rummage around the messy kitchen until I have found a dented soup pot, a metal cup, and two spoons. Treasure!

We return to the forest triumphant, Otto pushing the wheelbarrow, Mia riding with the potatoes, rubbing dirt into her hair. I carry the soup pot on my hip, a skip in my step.

Otto builds a fire, making sure to use only one of Alexi's precious matches. Mia hugs a potato to her chest.

I fill the soup pot with water from the brook and boil six potatoes for our dinner. Six big fat delicious potatoes!

We feast until we are full and Mia has started squishing cooked potato between her fingers. Then we sit by the fire, shoulder to shoulder, one blanket wrapped around us all. We are a Liesl-Mia-Otto-potato blob.

'That is the best dinner I've ever had,' says Otto.

'Really?' I ask.

'No, of course not!' he cries. 'I'm *pretending*, Liesl.' He waits a moment, then tries again. 'That is the best dinner I've ever had.'

'Me, too,' I reply, and smile at him. 'Even better than roast pork with sauerkraut.'

Otto grins. 'It was even better than roast pork with sauerkraut and gravy.'

I giggle. 'Even better than roast pork with sauerkraut and gravy and apple strudel for dessert.'

'Chocolate,' says Mia.

'Yes!' Otto springs to his feet and shouts, 'Even better than roast pork with sauerkraut and gravy and apple strudel with bucketloads of whipped cream for dessert, all washed down with hot chocolate!'

Mia starts to sing. She rocks a potato back and forth in her arms as though it is a baby.

'What is she singing?' Otto asks me.

'A nursery rhyme,' I say. 'A Russian nursery rhyme.' My voice drops. 'Captain Sokolov taught it to her.'

Otto sits down and pulls Mia into his lap. He takes the potato gently from her hands and rolls it away. Then he rocks her back and forth in his arms like a potato and sings her to sleep.

Otto sings Mia to sleep with a German lullaby about moonlight and roses. Soon Mia is snoring.

'Listen!' he whispers.

'What?' I ask.

'Mia is snoring in German.'

CHAPTER 27

We are sick of potatoes.

Four days and we've eaten nothing but potatoes. No matter how hard we try, we can no longer pretend that they taste like roast pork or apple strudel. They just taste like potatoes.

And then they begin to taste like sweaters or pillows or socks.

And then I begin to *wish* I were eating sweaters or pillows or socks. *Anything* other than potatoes.

Worst of all, even though we've eaten more potatoes than a pen full of pigs, we are still hungry.

'We need more food,' I say. 'Different food. Meat or fruit.'

'Or eggs,' says Otto. 'Mia loves eggs.'

'Brilliant!' I cry. '*Birds* lay eggs!'

'*Everyone* knows that,' scoffs Otto. 'Even Mia knows that.'

'But don't you see?' I throw my arms wide. 'We're in a forest. There are birds in a forest. And birds lay eggs. Especially in the springtime!'

Otto grins.

We go on an egg hunt. We wander through the forest, looking up into the trees. We stumble and trip and run into fallen logs, but it's worth it because, at last, Mia squeals, 'Mia see bird. Woof! Woof!'

Otto climbs up the tree trunk and along the branch. The poor mother bird squawks, then flaps about shrieking. I cannot bear to watch. Poor thing. We are about to steal her babies.

I take Mia by the hand and lead her to a patch of moss.

I rub her fingers across the cool green fuzz.

The bird falls silent, and I know that she has flown away. A tear runs down my cheek and drips onto the moss. We have become so wicked. I stand by Mia and the moss and weep silently.

I wonder if birds cry. Even if they don't shed tears, I'm sure the mother bird is weeping her heart out.

Now Otto is standing back at my side and he, too, is weeping. I hug him.

He sobs, great gasps that come from deep within his body. I think he is feeling guilty—cruel, wicked, dirty. Just like me.

Finally, he bellows, 'I found four eggs . . . uh . . . uh . . . Four big eggs . . . uh . . . uh . . . but I . . . but I . . .' He holds his empty hands out for me to see.

'You left them,' I whisper. 'You couldn't bear to take them from their poor mama.'

'Nooo!' howls Otto. 'I *ate* them! I gobbled them all myself!' He covers his face with his filthy hands and cries, 'Sorry, Liesl! Sorry, Mia! I am a bad selfish boy, but I was so hungry and they were so big and fat and round and I only meant to eat one but it was warm and gooey and so really truly delicious after all those potatoes, so I ate a second egg, and I thought, I will save the other two for my sisters, but they just seemed to jump into my mouth and now they are all gone!'

I want to scold him. I want to tell him how hungry I am. I want to remind him that Mia is a baby and needs lots of good food to grow. I want to shake him by the shoulders and yell in his face.

But I can't. He is heartbroken, and I am so hungry that I don't have the energy.

I sigh. 'Come on. We have two potatoes left. We'll eat, and then we'll find another house to raid.'

We take a different path through the forest this afternoon. None of us can bear to return to the potato farm. We sneak into a village, but we don't need to, because no one is living here. We walk along the cobbled street, looking through broken windows.

'It's a ghost town,' I murmur.

'Where is everyone?' asks Otto.

I think of the crammed roads as we were running from

our own village, the crowded barns at night, the stream of people trying to make it across the Vistula Lagoon to the ships that would take them far, far away.

'Gone,' I say. I look around at the empty street. There's not a dog or a cat to be seen, not even a chicken scratching between the cobblestones. 'They're all gone.'

'Forever?' asks Otto.

'No, of course not!' I snap. 'East Prussia is their home.' But I have to bite my lip to stop myself from crying.

Because why would they come back? There's nothing left but burned and broken homes. And a few forgotten potatoes.

'Come on,' says Otto. 'Let's not waste time in case there are smelly Russians nearby.'

We dash from house to house. The larders are empty. The blankets, clothes, and boots are all gone. The villagers must have taken everything when they fled. Or maybe the Russians came in after and stripped the village bare. But we scrounge and scrape up bits and pieces as we go: a smoked sausage that has rolled beneath a dresser, a box of matches dropped between hearthstones, two lettuces that have sprouted in an overgrown vegetable patch, grains of rice spilled across the floor—enough to fill Mia's pocket when I sweep them up. A feast!

'Let's go,' I say.

'Just one more house,' says Otto. 'My boots are rubbing. Maybe the last house will have shoes and socks. Maybe it will have a larder full of chocolate.'

Mia is half asleep on my back but still manages to murmur, 'Chocolate.'

How can I say no?

The last house is as bare as the others, but there's a barn out the back, and even though there are no animals, there is a bin full of oats.

'Horse food,' says Otto.

'People food now,' I cry. 'Porridge for breakfast!'

'Porridge!' Otto grins. 'That's almost as good as chocolate.'

'And it's not potatoes,' I add.

I'm scooping out the oats with my hands, filling our pockets, when the door flies open. I'm blinded by the sunlight, but I can see the silhouette of three people. I grab Mia and lift her into my arms before I notice that they are small people. Children, like us. Boys.

'Those are *our* oats,' snarls the oldest. He stomps forward, his hands balled into fists.

'Is this your house?' asks Otto.

'No,' says the second boy, 'but those are *our* oats.'

The three boys stand before us. They are thin, dirty, ragged. They look angry, dangerous, ready to fight.

I think I could knock the biggest boy over if I had to, but there are three of them and only two of us. Mia doesn't count because she's just a baby.

Our pockets are already full, so I say, 'We're sorry. We didn't know the oats belonged to you.' I step away from the bin and pull Otto with me.

The biggest boy nods and his hands open. No more fists.
'Where are you hiding?' he asks.

'How do you know we're hiding?' I reply. He snorts and
waits for me to answer. 'The forest,' I say. Otto points.

'Your mama?' the biggest boy asks.

Nobody asks about papas in a war. They are all gone—
fighting or lost.

I shake my head.

'You're on your own,' says the boy, 'like all the other children running around the forests and villages without anyone
to look after them. You're living wild. Like wolves. Like animals. Like us.'

'Wild children,' I murmur. 'Wolf children.'

I stare at the three boys. They are definitely wild. They
are so filthy that it's hard to see where their clothes end and
their skin starts. The youngest boy has a deep cut on his cheek,
and the blood hasn't been cleaned away. He has a scared look
in his eyes, like Mozart had when the rockets started falling
on the ice.

Mia presses her head into my cheek, and I smell her hair.
It stinks. I look at Otto and notice how thick the dirt is on his
hands and face.

We look like these boys! We are living like these boys. But
we have no choice. And we are not wild. I *refuse* to let Otto
and Mia become wolves. Mama would not like it. Papa would
not like it. Oma and Opa would not like it.

'We are not wild!' I snap.

The biggest boy shrugs. He reaches down into the barrel, grabs some oats, and shoves them into his mouth.

'Hitler is dead,' says the middle boy.

'Liar!' I hiss. What a wicked thing to say.

But he insists. 'Truly.'

'Liar!' I shout.

I open my mouth to say it again, but I can't, because the youngest boy—skinny, bloody, scared—reminds me of the soldiers that straggled through our village the day Mama and I bought the Christmas goose with her pearls. I think of the jeeps and trucks and tanks that once belonged to the glorious German Army, but now sit broken and rusting in the fields; the burned and broken villages; the Russians swarming all over East Prussia; the empty houses we have just searched; and these boys and Mia and Otto and me, all alone without mamas or papas or anyone to care for us. What does it matter whether Hitler is alive or dead? Hitler is not here and he is not helping. Not one little bit.

'Hitler is a swine,' Otto says.

'A *dead* swine,' corrects the middle boy.

'Yeah,' smirks the biggest boy. 'Hitler is a dead swine and the war is over. We lost.'

CHAPTER 28

The three boys are right. Hitler is dead. Germany has lost the war.

There have been no victory parades with bars of chocolate tossed into the crowd, no fountains flowing with lemonade, no new boots or pretty dresses with satin ribbons tied around the waist, no sausage-dog puppies filling our home with their flapping ears and yapping.

There's not even a home. There's just a Liesl-Mia-Otto huddle amid a pile of blankets beneath the shelter of a tree.

But those three boys were wrong about one thing. We are not wild. We are not turning into wolves. I will not let it happen. Mama would be so disappointed.

'We are not wild,' I tell Mia and Otto every single day. 'We are not wolves.'

We lie by a creek for hours, watching, waiting for the

crayfish to crawl by. We dive, grab, toss the crayfish onto the bank, and roar like savages, 'Dinner! Dinner! Crayfish for dinner!'

But as I boil the crayfish and we eat them, guts and all, I remind Mia and Otto and even myself, 'We are not wild. We are not wolves.'

We forage through the forest and along the edges of the lakes for strawberries, blueberries, and raspberries. We are so starving hungry that we stuff them into our mouths straight from the bushes. We grin at each other, our lips and chins covered with juice, the cracks between our teeth a mush of pulp and seeds. Purple and red. Sticky and stained.

I laugh as Mia rubs raspberries into her smelly, matted hair, then say, 'Enough, Mia. We are not wild. We are not wolves.' A few people return to their homes—East Prussians who have fled but now creep back. Others move into houses and buildings that are not their own. They work for the Russians and grow vegetables and keep a few sickly animals. They are trying to rebuild their lives from nothing in a land that is no longer theirs. They do not have a scrap to spare for children living alone in the forest.

We hide behind barns, and when farmers go into their houses, we steal the slops from the pig troughs, the eggs from the nesting boxes. We break into kitchens and gobble whole pots of soup while the wife is outside doing the laundry. But even as we run from the house, curses being hurled at us from the clothesline, I tell myself, *We are just trying to survive. We are not wild. We are not wolves.*

Today, we steal a hen. It's a Russian hen. We know it's Russian because, as we run away from the barn, two Russian soldiers yell and shoot at us as we disappear into the forest. Real bullets whiz past our bodies.

We laugh and scream and cry all at the same time as we run and dive into the deep, dark undergrowth. We have become bold and brave. Or bold and reckless. Or maybe we have gone mad.

I am so hungry, so desperate for meat, that I wring the hen's neck before we get back to our camp and I don't even cry.

Mia claps and shouts, 'Mia love chicken! Yum!'

She is speaking so well and I am proud of her words, but I am also scared because being always hungry has made her heartless. It is the same for Otto and me. Food comes first.

I roast the chicken over a fire, and we eat it all—bones, heart, lungs, kidneys, brain, and feet. Chicken feet are delicious. Otto even eats the eyes.

When we are done, and we are lying on our greasy blankets beneath the summer sky, half naked in our torn clothes, our feet bare, their soles grown thick and tough from running about without boots, I remind Mia and Otto and myself once more, 'We are not wild. We are not wolves.'

'I'd *like* to be a wolf,' says Otto.

'Wolves don't roast chicken,' I remind him. 'They eat it raw.'

'I don't care,' says Otto. 'I've eaten raw frogs, raw slugs. I even ate a crayfish straight from the creek when you weren't looking.'

'Wolves don't live in houses!' I snap.

'*We* don't live in a house,' says Otto. 'Not anymore.'

A ladybug crawls across my face and settles on the tip of my nose. I'm losing this argument.

'Wolves don't sing lullabies and tell bedtime stories,' I point out.

'*We* don't tell bedtime stories anymore,' Otto retorts.

I prop myself on my elbow and lock eyes with him. 'Once upon a time,' I begin in a loud, bossy voice. I hesitate. 'Once upon a time . . .'

I don't know how to go on. We haven't had a bedtime story since we left home. We've been too tired. Too scared. Too hungry. And there's no Mama to hold it all together— the words, the dreams, the cuddles, the happily-ever-after.

'Go on,' whispers Otto, his eyes now wide and eager.

But what do I say? There can be no brave Otto marching across the kingdom, defeating the Red Army. And I don't want to fill our forest with wicked witches and strange enchantments. It's already bad enough to be living here without imagining such horrid things.

I try again. 'Once upon a time . . .' My chest aches. Mia sticks a chicken feather up her nose and sneezes.

I laugh. 'Once upon a time, there was a princess called Mia.'

'Mia *love* chicken,' sings Mia.

'Yes!' I cry. 'Princess Mia *loved* to eat roast chicken, and . . . and . . .'

'And she had a magic calf called Dog!' shouts Otto.

We are silent for a moment as we remember Dog, which makes us think of Dmitri and Alexi. My story is in danger of ending in tears, so I blunder on.

'Dog's magic power was that everything he touched with his nose turned to food.'

Otto nods and says, 'Dog pressed his nose against a schoolbook and it turned into a roast chicken.'

'And then,' I continue, 'he poked his nose into a pile of pebbles and they turned into roast potatoes with crispy golden skins and gravy drizzled all over!'

Mia claps her hands and shouts, 'Mia eat tatoes!'

Otto and I beam at her. Clever girl! She's helping us with our story.

'Dog poked his nose at the king's boots,' I say, 'and they turned into chocolate! "Chocolate boots!" roared the king. "But they will melt all over my royal feet!"'

Mia squeals with delight. 'Mia love chocolate!'

'I know!' I cry. 'Princess Mia loved chocolate so much that she gobbled the king's boots *right off his feet*.'

'And *then* she burped!' shouts Otto.

He burps to demonstrate, and I burp too, and Mia tries,

but blows snot from her nose instead. We all burst out laughing.

Soon we are burping and squealing and rolling around with pine needles tangled in our hair, a Mia-Otto-Liesl blob of happiness and sunshine and full bellies and snot and love.

And I think we really are like three wild wolf pups tumbling about on the forest floor. But I don't remind Mia and Otto that we are not wild. That we are not wolves.

Because sometimes it's good to be wild. Sometimes you *have* to be wild.

CHAPTER 29

I wake feeling scared. Mia is clinging to me.

Someone is leaning over us. A child. I cannot tell whether it's a boy or a girl. I stare into two big brown eyes set in a dirty, thin face.

'Go away,' I croak.

The child spits at me, steps back, and says something in Russian. Something rude—words I learned from the Red Army soldiers when I was their potato-peeling prisoner.

I sit up. Another child, a big boy, is stealing our wheelbarrow.

'Hey!' I shout. 'That's ours!' Otto wakes and sits up.

Both children shout at us in Russian. The boy grabs our soup pot and throws it at us. The other child throws rocks. One hits me on the side of my head.

Otto springs to his feet, but the boy picks up a big stick

and holds it as though he is used to handling a weapon.

'Don't, Otto,' I whisper. 'Let them go.' Otto sits back down.

The boy snarls. He drops the stick, grabs the wheelbarrow, and disappears into the forest. The other child runs forward, spits on us again, then scampers away.

'Wild children,' says Otto. 'Wolves.'

'Russian children,' I whisper. 'Russian wolves.'

I peel Mia from my body, wrap her in a blanket, and tuck her between the roots of the oak tree we call home.

'We have to move on,' I tell Otto. 'We're not safe here anymore. Russian children might come back with Russian soldiers.'

'I don't want to go,' he says. 'Mama might be catching up to us.'

He's right. How will Mama ever find us if we keep moving from place to place? My eyes prickle.

'Mama is clever,' I say. 'And she loves us. She'll keep looking.'

'But I like it here. I like our home.'

'I'll build us a new home,' I say. 'A better one. A proper one with a roof.'

'You don't even know *how* to build,' says Otto.

'I'll learn,' I retort. 'I didn't know how to kill a chicken until I tried.'

'You are good at killing chickens,' he admits. I blush. But not because I'm proud.

We trudge out of the forest and around a lake. I try to remember when we last washed. Weeks ago? Months ago? It's not easy to get excited about bathing when the water is icy and there are no towels or warm fluffy nightdresses to slip into when you're done. But today is a hot summer's day, and the water is clean and clear.

'Let's bathe!' I say.

I undress, then peel off Mia's crusty clothes. She screams when I carry her into the lake. She's not used to feeling cool water all around her body. But I hold her tightly and sing her German nursery rhymes and dance about until she settles.

I wash the dirt from her skin, then Otto and I take it in turns to swirl her through the water by her arms. Her eyes are wide, but soon she is smiling and splashing and even laughing.

I scrub our clothes and spread them over the bushes to dry. We sit naked on the rocks at the edge of the lake and soak up the sunshine.

Mia looks pretty now that the dirt is gone. Even though her hair is still knotted like a doormat. Even though her ribs and elbows and knees look too big for her skin. Otto too is all sharp edges and knobbly joints where the chubbiness used to be.

We sit in silence until the rumbling of our tummies grows too loud to bear.

We dress and walk on, following a stream that runs into a new forest. We wander through thick green shade until we reach a clearing where the sun shines down upon a blanket of yellow wildflowers. It is beautiful, like something from a storybook. Fairies would like to live here. Princesses. Magic calves.

I run into the middle of the flowers and spin around and around. Mia mimics me, spinning until she falls down into the flowers. She rolls about, giggling, babbling. She presses her pale little face to the ground and kisses the flowers. When she sits up, her lips are gold with pollen.

Trees form a thick ring around the glade. There is plenty of shelter. There are clumps of bushes where we can hide. There is fresh water from the stream, and a little pond where we can bathe. There is light and loveliness.

'Here!' I announce. 'Here's where we will build our house.'

'There!' shouts Otto. 'There's already a house!'

The house is not really a house. It's an old woodcutter's hut. So old that the timber is rotting, and it leans to one side as though it might fall down at any moment. But old is good because it means that nobody uses it anymore. And to us, it is a palace.

We creep inside and find ourselves staring at an owl. It blinks but does not move.

'Helloo!' sings Mia. She opens and closes her hands in a baby wave.

'Hoo! Hoo!' says the owl.

Mia squeals. 'Mia love bird. Woof! Woof!'

'Hoo! Hoo!' repeats the owl.

'Woof! Woof!' says Mia once more, as though correcting it.

Otto licks his lips and narrows his eyes. He makes a dash for the owl, but it flies up through a hole in the roof and escapes.

My tummy rumbles, but I am glad. How could we eat a wise old owl? It would be like eating one of the good, kind creatures from a storybook. I'd feel like a troll or a big bad wolf or a wicked witch. I will not be a wicked witch!

But suddenly all I can think about is roast owl, with Mama's bread-and-currant stuffing and cranberry sauce. My mouth fills with saliva and my tummy rumbles again. Harder, longer, louder. And I know that I could eat a wise old owl or a fluffy little rabbit or even a sausage dog, if only I could get my hands on one.

'Mia love bird!' says Mia. 'Yum! Yum!'

I sigh. We *are* wild. We *are* wolves.

I stand in front of the hut. The wildflowers bend and wave around my bare legs as a warm afternoon breeze lolls by. *Think of something other than roast owl,* I tell myself.

My tummy rumbles, and now the roast owl is sitting on a platter surrounded by roast potatoes, roast parsnips, and roast carrots.

Think about the carrots, I tell myself. *You hate carrots. Carrots make you sick.*

But these ones don't. They have a huge knob of butter

melting on top, and they look delicious. I would gobble them in a heartbeat.

I wander away from the hut and find a clump of dandelions. I remember a book we read at school about foraging in the forest.

'Dandelions make a pleasing addition to any soup or salad,' I say, quoting the line that seemed so silly when I first read it. Now the words are magic.

I pick a leaf and chew on it. It doesn't taste *pleasing* at all, but as though I've picked a weed from the garden and stuck it in my mouth. I grimace, chew, and swallow, then pick a second leaf.

The grass in front of me rustles. I freeze.

I lean forward, and a big brown hare leaps out. This time I don't think how sweet the hare looks, or how sad it would be to eat something I've seen in picture books. I shout, 'Supper!'

It's a stupid thing to shout. I should have shouted, 'Hare!' But Otto knows it's the same thing and comes running, a grin on his lips, a glint in his eyes.

I chase the hare until it dives into a bush. 'In there!' I gasp as Otto catches up to me.

Otto runs to the far side of the bush. We stare at one another. I nod and we both leap in.

Sticks tear at my face and arms, Otto swears, the hare squeals, and the bush shakes. I don't know how he does it, but Otto emerges holding the dead hare by its ears.

'Supper!' he roars, holding it in the air like a trophy. 'Supper!' I shout, and thrust my own hands in the air.

I stare at Otto—the twigs and leaves in his hair, the blood dripping from the cuts on his hands and face, the tear in his shirt. Otto stares back at me, and I know I must look the same. We burst out laughing.

I turn around to see if Mia has caught up to us, but she hasn't. We walk back to our new house, but Mia is nowhere in sight. Perhaps she's lying down in the flowers, painting her entire body with the golden flecks of pollen.

'Mia!' I call. 'We have supper!' She does not answer.

'Mia!' shouts Otto, waving the hare around once more. 'Yum yums for Mia. Woof! Woof!' He thinks it's so funny, he says it again, but when Mia doesn't answer, he falls silent.

Otto tosses the hare into the hut and we run back and forth across the clearing, calling, shouting, begging for Mia to come out from wherever she's hiding. But she doesn't come out. She is nowhere to be seen.

'She must be in the forest,' I cry.

Otto spins around, looking at the thick wall of trees that surrounds the clearing. 'But where?' he whispers.

'I don't know!' I shout. 'Just look!'

I stride toward the forest and stop. I turn around and head in the opposite direction, but it feels foolish, because it's just a guess. So many trees to choose from. Millions of them. Why would Mia be hiding behind one tree instead of any other?

I run back to Otto and open my mouth to speak, but nothing comes out.

'We've lost Mia,' cries Otto. 'And we promised Mama that we would stick together. It's our fault for chasing the hare!'

My throat is so tight I can't even speak. But Otto is talking enough for both of us.

'No,' he says. 'It's not our fault. It's Hitler's fault. Hitler started the war and lost it, and now we have no proper home, no proper supper, no Mama, no Papa . . . and no little sister.' He runs to the middle of the clearing and bellows, 'I hate Hitler!'

He screams it over and over again. And it's a good thing that he's screaming because, eventually, somebody hears.

A dark figure steps out from the trees. It's carrying a bundle in its arms. As the figure comes nearer, we see that it's a tall, skinny, dirty boy.

The bundle wriggles.

'Hello.' The boy nods and smiles.

The bundle turns toward us and sings out, 'Mia hungry. Woof! Woof!'

CHAPTER 30

Karl is a big boy, fourteen, and he's very good at skinning a hare. He has a pocketknife and strong hands, and he doesn't even gag when the intestines slip out onto the dirt like a giant purple worm. He spreads the fur on the roof of the hut and tells Mia that when it dries, he will make it into a toy rabbit. Mia claps her hands and sings, 'Mia love rabbit. Yum! Yum!'

We all laugh but I feel sad inside. Mia should have enough food and enough toys so that she doesn't get confused between the two.

We sit around the fire, drooling as the lid on the soup pot bounces up and down, letting little wafts of steam escape. The smell is making me dribble. I've never made hare-and-dandelion soup before, but I know it will be delicious.

'Are you like us?' Otto asks Karl.

'What do you mean?' says Karl.

'A child without a mama or a papa or any other grown-up to look after them,' I explain. 'A child living wild—stealing, hunting, doing bad things to survive.'

Karl nods. He doesn't even think about it.

'We saw wild *Russian* children,' says Otto.

'I've seen them too,' says Karl. 'They're orphans who followed the Red Army from Russia into East Prussia. They go into houses, farms, and villages after the Red Army soldiers have been there and take the leftovers. I suppose they're just trying to survive, like the rest of us.'

'They hit Liesl with a rock,' says Otto.

'And stole our wheelbarrow,' I add. A sore head will heal, but a stolen wheelbarrow is gone forever.

'How did you lose *your* mama?' asks Otto.

Karl rubs his eyes. 'I didn't lose my mama. I ran away.'

Karl is stupid. Really, *really* stupid. Doesn't he know that children *need* their mamas? Doesn't he know that children especially need their mamas when there are Russian soldiers doing bad things all over East Prussia? Doesn't he know that children like me would do *anything* to be with a mama who loves them?

But I don't say it. It seems rude. Especially after he rescued Mia and skinned the hare. Instead, Otto and I stare at him and wait.

Karl squirms, then shrugs. 'Before I ran away,' he says, 'I was in the Hitler Youth. Each day after school I marched, did fitness classes and hand-to-hand combat, and sang with other boys my age. On the weekends we went for bike rides and long hikes through meadows and forests. In the summer holidays we had camping trips where we learned how to make fires, build shelters, hide in trees, splint a broken leg, use the sun and the stars to find our way home.'

'It sounds fun,' I say.

'It was.' Karl frowns. 'But sometimes I think Hitler made us learn all those things because he *knew* that one day we would be living like this, in the woods, surviving on our own after Germany had been beaten by the rest of the world.'

My skin prickles at such dangerous talk. But Hitler is dead, and who is there to hear?

'But you're right,' says Karl. 'It *was* fun. I was proud to be a Hitler Youth. But then . . .' His chin drops and his voice drops with it. 'Then I was asked to do something bad—me and some other Hitler Youth from my village. They gave us brandy to drink.'

'That's terrible!' gasps Otto. 'Children shouldn't drink brandy.'

'They gave us guns,' Karl continues. 'Real guns, with bullets.'

'That's even worse!' shouts Otto. 'Children shouldn't have guns.'

'And they told us that there were prisoners, Jewish women, and girls . . .'

He can't go on. He covers his face with his hands, and

even though he is a big, tall fourteen-year-old boy, he begins to cry.

I don't want to hear this story. It can't possibly end with a happily-ever-after.

I put my hand on Karl's shoulder. 'You are just a boy,' I say. 'They made you do it.'

'No!' he shouts, shrugging my hand off. 'I *didn't* do it! I ran away. I threw the gun at the nearest SS officer, and I ran as far away from the village as I could. And I didn't go back, because I knew I'd get into trouble for disobeying orders. And now that the war is over, I still can't go back because the people will think that I *did* that terrible thing, and I didn't!'

Otto is scrunching his nose and scratching his knees. He doesn't understand what the terrible thing is. At least, I *hope* he doesn't.

But I understand. I wish I didn't.

I feel sick. And sad.

And angry.

I'm so confused, I don't know what to say. So I take Karl's hand and cry along with him.

CHAPTER 31

We ask Karl to stay because he's big and strong and has a knife, and we like him. Besides, he has nowhere else to go.

He teaches Otto how to use the stars and the sun and the moss on the tree trunks to follow a straight path and make sure he never gets lost. He teaches me about mushrooms—the ones we can eat and the ones that are poisonous. My stomach drops when he tells us we must never eat raw slugs, that they could kill us.

Karl makes a toy rabbit from the hare skin for Mia. It is the ugliest toy I have ever seen, with sticks for legs and a misshapen head, but Mia loves it. She calls it Baby and carries it with her everywhere.

Otto and Karl patch the roof of the hut with twigs and moss. I stick our two family photos onto the wall, and I get

Mia to point to the people and name them—Mama, Papa, Oma, Opa. She is only little, and I do not want her to forget. Our days slip into a pattern. When we have all woken, we fold the blankets as though Mama is standing over us, telling us to make our beds, and then we go hunting.

Sometimes we forage in the forest and along the stream, finding mushrooms, wild sorrel, dandelions, berries, frogs, tadpoles, crayfish, worms. Sometimes we venture onto farms or into villages, scavenging or stealing. But food is growing more and more scarce, and where there is food, there are people, and they don't want to share the little they have. Everyone is trying to survive. Everyone is mean.

If we have good hunting, the afternoon is spent cooking, eating, and digesting. We lie in the sun, patting our bellies, pretending they're full even though there's never enough to take the hunger away. We imagine the frog we shared was a schnitzel, the withered berries we ate were gingerbread men, the boiled water with dandelions was pea soup, thick and salty with butter melting on top.

If we have bad hunting, the afternoon is spent bathing, resting, lying in the sun, and pretending that tomorrow we will find a feast.

The hunger is always there, a monster clawing at our bellies, nagging, sometimes howling. Always, always, we are thinking about food. We want more. We need more. And the need makes us foolish.

Otto crosses a minefield to pick blackberries. He zigzags

between the mounds of dirt, running, dodging, skipping. He takes off his shirt and turns it into a pouch that he fills with the precious, plump blackberries, then he zigzags back. We are laughing, shoving berries into our mouths and slapping him on the shoulder, when a crow lands in the field and explodes. Clods of dirt rain down upon our heads, and all that remains of the crow is one black feather fluttering through the air. Foolish.

I steal duck eggs at a train station in the middle of the day. I don't know who owns the ducks or why their cages are just sitting at the side of the track, but I don't care. The ducks don't care either. I find a bucket in the restroom and steal all the eggs from beneath the feathery bottoms. I want to steal the ducks, too, but when I grab them, they quack and flap and make such a fuss that I think I'll get caught. I jump back in fright, and they leap out the open cage doors, waddle onto the train track, then take flight. My heart gives a little flit. I'm glad they're free. And then my tummy also gives a little flit because, if we're lucky, they might fly into our clearing one day and waddle through the wildflowers, and then we can have roast duck for supper!

Karl steals from the Red Army. He finds a house on the edge of a village where Russian soldiers are living, eating, drinking, sleeping. He watches for three days, and when he's sure they're all asleep, he raids. He steals a loaf of bread, a sack of potatoes, bandages, a pair of boots, a helmet, and a gun. We feast until our tummies are truly full.

Otto clomps around in the boots. They're far too big, but he pads them with grass, and they're better than running around barefoot as he's had to do for the last month. Mia uses the helmet as a bed for Baby.

I throw the gun in the lake.

'Why did you do that?' asks Karl.

'I don't want it near Mia or Otto,' I say. 'Little children shouldn't touch guns.' I put my hands on my hips. '*Big* children shouldn't touch guns.'

Karl blushes. I know he's remembering the women and the girls and the horrible thing he was told to do. And I feel sorry for him, I truly do. But I am cross and I cannot stop myself.

'In fact,' I am now shouting, '*adults* shouldn't touch guns either! If nobody touched guns, there'd be no war!'

'Yes, there would,' mutters Karl. 'They'd just use sticks and stones instead. People always find a way to fight.'

Perhaps he's right. But I'm still glad I threw the gun away.

Otto and Mia play with the Russian bandages. Otto gets Mia to limp about pretending she has a broken leg. He winds a bandage around and around her leg, pats her on the head, and says, 'All better now, little calf.'

Mia holds up her finger and cries, 'Ouch!'

Otto bandages her finger, her hand, and her entire arm. Mia smiles, pats him on the head, and says, 'Otto all better now.'

Otto laughs, hugs Mia, and declares, 'I'm going to be a vet when I grow up!'

I frown. I don't think there'll be any animals left in East Prussia by the time Otto grows up. They'll all have been stolen by the Russians or eaten by starving East Prussians.

Even Otto would gladly eat an injured animal rather than fix it up. Still, it makes me happy that he can dream about a future where life can be normal once more.

But my happiness quickly turns to worry. Vets must go to university, and Otto hasn't yet made it through the second grade. How will he ever be smart enough to be a vet if he doesn't go to school? He won't even be smart enough to write a letter or read the newspapers.

Then my worry turns to anger. 'Guns and land mines instead of books and desks!' I shout. 'It's all so wrong!'

I want to kick something. The soup pot catches my eye, and I stride toward it. But before I kick, a better idea springs to mind.

I grab the soup pot and slam it down on the ground in front of Otto. 'Say good afternoon to Fräulein Hofmann.'

Otto scrunches his nose.

'Do it!' I shout.

Otto looks at me as though I'm crazy, but then he drones, just as he would at school, 'Good afternoon, Fräulein Hofmann.'

'Now,' I say, 'let's sing our five times table.'

And we do. And Karl joins in, and even Mia in her own special way. And so the Forest School for Wild Children begins.

Fräulein Hofmann the soup pot is in charge, but Karl and

I are her helpers. I worry that Otto will be too tired and too hungry to learn, but as long as he's staring into the sky, adding twenty-five and ten together in his head, he's not thinking of food. He quickly grows used to spelling out loud, singing his way through all of the times tables, and recalling important dates in German history.

Mia sorts rocks, sticks, and wildflowers into groups. She draws in the mud with her fingers and learns actions to go with her favorite German nursery rhymes.

Karl collects charcoal from the fire and makes me do long division on the rocks by the lake. He laughs when I get it wrong, and when I get it right, he hugs me.

The first time I blush and pull away. The second time I smile. After that, I hug him back every time.

'What about Karl?' asks Otto. 'When is *he* going to do some lessons?'

It's a good question, but Karl is older than us, so he's already done all the lessons we know.

'We need books,' I say.

But books don't grow on trees. If they did, we would be surrounded by a forest full of lovely things to read.

'What's that?' Karl asks, cupping his ear and leaning in toward the soup pot. 'Fräulein Hofmann says she knows just the place to find books.'

The church stands alone on a hill. The entrance has been blasted to bits, there's an old tank rusting away where it was driven through the wall, there's a gaping hole in the roof, and most of the windows are missing. The candlesticks, the candles, the chalice, and all the lace cloths have been taken. But there is one perfect stained-glass window, small, bright, and beautiful, with the sun shining through. A little miracle. A little treasure.

Mia and I stand before the window, staring. It's a picture of David, the shepherd boy, smiling down at a lamb.

'Woof! Woof!' says Mia. She waves at the lamb.

'It's a sheep,' says Otto. 'Baa! Baa!'

'Baa! Baa!' echoes Mia.

My tummy rumbles. I am dreaming of roast lamb with rosemary. What would David, the shepherd boy, say if he knew that I was thinking about eating his favorite lamb? My cheeks burn with shame.

Karl leads us through a door into a side room. The big church Bible has been tossed and trampled on the floor. What a wicked thing to do! Even worse than wanting to eat David's favorite lamb.

I kneel down and try to separate the muddy pages. 'There might be bits left that we can still read,' I say.

'No need,' says Karl. 'Look!'

He opens a cupboard to reveal three neat rows of books, all with fine leather covers, crimson, tan, and black. There are German hymnbooks, Lutheran prayer books, and Bibles.

'Perfect!' I shout.

Even though there are many copies of just the three books, we take as many as we can carry. Books are treasure.

Every day now, Fräulein Hofmann the soup pot gets us to sing a hymn, read three prayers, recite all of the times tables, and read stories from the Bible.

Karl is made to read the parts with the long, difficult names—Nebuchadnezzar, Abimelech, Maher-shalal-hash-baz. He laughs as he bumbles through the astonishing names, and we all laugh with him.

Otto gets to read the same story over and over again until he knows all the words and can read with expression.

Mia pretends to read to Baby, babbling on about dogs and sheep and cows that all say, 'Woof! Woof!'

I'm not sure that the Bible, the hymnbook, and the prayer book can teach Otto everything he needs to become a vet. But our lessons are fun, and they fill the long, hungry afternoons.

And the paper from the extra books we have stolen is light, thin, and dry, perfect for lighting fires and wiping bottoms.

CHAPTER 32

Fräulein Hofmann takes us to the lake for today's lessons. We are just settling her on a large rock when we realize that we're not alone. Two boys are fishing a small distance away. My mouth waters at the thought of fried fish, and our books slip from my hands onto the grass.

'We'd better go, Liesl,' whispers Karl, grabbing my arm. 'We don't know if they'll be kind or mean.'

'Or if they're German or Russian,' adds Otto.

'Hellooooo!' One of the boys has spotted us and is waving. The other boy starts reeling in his fishing line.

'Fish,' I sigh. 'Fresh fish.'

I can't help myself. I walk toward them, eyes fixed upon the point where the line disappears beneath the water.

The boy with the fishing rod steps forward onto a rock and slips. His foot splashes into the water, but the second boy grabs his arm and keeps him from falling in. They both laugh.

Kind boys, I think. *Happy boys.* And I keep walking until I'm right beside them.

I watch in wonder as they pull a large striped fish from the water and toss it onto the grass. It flips and flounders about, but I don't feel an ounce of pity, just a giant rumble in my tummy.

I don't know how long I stare and drool at the fish, but when I turn to the boys, they are both grinning at me.

'Hungry?' asks the tallest. I nod.

He steps forward, uses a knife to kill the fish, and hands it to me.

'It's a perch,' he says. 'Good eating.'

I stare at the fish in my hands. I open and close my mouth, like the fish was doing just seconds ago. I clutch it to my chest, then burst out crying. I am overwhelmed by the simple kindness of this boy and the idea that this fish has just landed in my hands like a gift from a fairy godmother.

Bruno is eleven and has stringy brown hair and green eyes. Josef is ten and has a shaved head and blue eyes.

'Lice,' he says as he runs his hand across the short blond prickles. 'Easiest way to get rid of them.'

Bruno and Josef are wild children. Like us. But not like us.

They are skinny, with dirty faces and tattered clothes, but they have a shine in their eyes and an energy that can only come from eating proper food. Not bugs and frogs and weeds.

'Where do you live?' asks Otto.

Bruno points to the far side of the lake. 'Over there, past the next bit of forest, in a barn.'

'Aren't you scared of the Russians catching you?' I ask.

'Too late!' says Bruno. 'The barn is on our farm. The Russian soldiers arrived before we had time to run away. They moved into our house and made Mama cook and clean for them, and they sent us out each day to catch fresh fish for their supper.'

'You have a *mama*!' I gasp, envy dripping from every word. A mama is even better than a fish.

Bruno shakes his head. 'One day a new Russian soldier came to the door and tried to take me away.' He wipes his eyes and nose on the back of his arm. 'He wanted me to help herd some cows . . . east . . . all the way to Russia. Mama screamed and said they couldn't take me because I was just a boy, so they took her instead.'

Josef says, 'They're taking *all* the East Prussian cows to Russia, you know.'

I think Josef is talking about the cows so he doesn't have to think about his mama.

'I know,' I whisper.

I know about the cows. I also know about trying not to think of mamas and papas and omas and opas.

Bruno stares at the ground. 'They sent our mama away and told us we could stay in the barn if we did our mama's housework as well as catching the fresh fish for their supper.'

'You're their slaves,' says Karl.

'It's not so bad,' Josef says. 'We *like* fishing!'

Again, I think he's talking about the fish so that he doesn't have to think about his mama.

Bruno nods. '*And* they give us food.'

Food! Russian food! I think of Viktor's bricks of warm bread, his chunky potato soup, his honey cake. Lucky boys. That explains their bright eyes and sharp, sure movements. *We* move like slugs.

Josef pulls a worm from his pocket, threads it onto his hook, and casts his line out into the lake once more.

My eyes and mouth grow wide. He's hoping to catch another fish. Imagine! *Two* fish for supper! We haven't had anything better than the worm for days.

'Aren't you scared?' Otto asks Bruno. 'Don't you hate the Russians?'

Bruno shrugs. 'It's better than starving or living in the forest.'

I glance at Karl. He's a tall, strong boy. He has no cute baby sister who might be kidnapped and sent back to Russia to a lonely wife. *He* could work for the Russians.

The idea of Karl leaving us puts a sudden ache in my chest.

But Karl doesn't seem interested. He gathers wood and makes a fire, then sings nursery rhymes with Mia. She's too tired to do the actions, so Karl does them for her, smiling all the time. He is so very kind.

Don't leave, Karl, I say over and over in my head.

Josef catches three more perch, and I cook *all* the fish in our soup pot. It's a feast. Well, not a feast, but we each have enough fish to fill our mouths several times over, and the meat sits in our tummies, making us feel full and happy.

We take Bruno and Josef back to our clearing and show them where we live. We splash in the stream, throw rocks in the pond, then lie down in the sunshine to digest the fish. I half doze, grass tickling my shoulders, Mia's snores burbling in my ear. A dream is starting to dance around the edge of my mind when Karl says, 'Should we read a story?' We all like the idea.

Karl flicks through the Bible. 'How about Jonah and the big fish? That's a good one to read for Bruno and Josef the fishermen.'

Bruno laughs. 'I like fish stories. Our mama used to tell us a story about a fish that swallowed a golden ring.'

'Our mama used to tell us a story about a fish who was an enchanted prince,' I say. 'He was able to grant wishes.'

'Let's make up our own story!' shouts Otto.

'In turns!' cries Karl. 'We'll go around the circle like we used to when we sat around the fire at night at . . . camp.' He blushes, and I know he's thinking about the Hitler Youth.

'Good idea,' I say, and give him my widest smile.

We shuffle into a circle—me, Karl, Bruno, Otto, and Josef. We make Mia a part too, even though she is still sound asleep. We sit with our hands on our knees, grinning at one another. It feels strange but fun. It's a game, and we haven't played a game since Dmitri and Alexi taught us Durak.

'I'll start,' I say. 'Once upon a time there was a magic fish—'

'Called Gustav!' cries Otto.

Josef giggles. 'Gustav is an excellent name for a fish.'

'Thank you,' says Otto.

'You're not doing it right,' says Karl. 'Stay in order.'

I clear my throat, give my best schoolteacher scowl, and begin again. 'Once upon a time there was a magic fish called Gustav.'

I tap Karl on the shoulder, and he continues.

'Gustav was a very happy fish. He spent his days swimming about in the lake and visiting the other fishies' homes, where they would eat gherkins and talk about the weather.'

Everyone stares at him.

'What?' says Karl. 'I *love* gherkins.'

'But this is a story,' I explain. 'Gustav the fish can eat anything in the world. Anything he likes. Anything *you* like!'

'I like gherkins,' says Karl. 'They're my favorite food.'

Otto, Josef, and Bruno clutch their tummies and moan.

Karl blushes but holds fast. 'Gustav definitely ate gherkins!'

'But *most* of the time,' says Otto, smirking and looking sideways at Karl, 'Gustav and his friends ate chocolate—'

'And apple strudel with cream,' adds Bruno.

'And almond cake!' shouts Josef.

The story has returned to me. 'Gustav was a very happy magic fish, until a big black bear called Josef caught him in his net. "Oho!" roared Josef. "What a tasty-looking fish! I will eat you for my supper." But Gustav wept and wailed and cried, "Oh, please, please, don't eat me. I am a magic fish, and if you set me free into the lake once more, I will grant you three wishes."'

'Five wishes!' shouts Karl. 'That way we can all say one.'

I frown at him.

'And I promise I won't use my wish to get gherkins,' he says.

I nod. 'All right. *Five* wishes. The bear agreed and released Gustav the magic fish back into the lake, and decided that he would use the first wish straightaway.'

I tap Karl on the shoulder.

Karl clears his throat and says, 'The bear growled, "I wish I had a giant pot of honey that would *never* run dry." And— POOF!—the pot of honey appeared in the bear's paws. He stuck his head in the pot and gobbled and slurped until he was so full that honey came out of his ears and ran down his shoulders, and *still* the honey came up to the brim of the pot.'

Bruno laughs until he snorts. 'I like that! I really, *really* like it! Honey coming out of his ears!' He laughs some more, then carries on with the story. 'The bear used his second wish the next day. He was walking through the woods when he stepped in a trap and it closed around his leg. "Ouch! Ouch!"

he cried. "I wish I was free and that the nasty hunter who set this trap was caught in it himself." And—POOF!—the bear was free and the hunter was trapped instead. The bear licked his lips. He wrapped a big red napkin around his neck, pulled out a knife and fork, and gobbled the hunter up for supper.'

We all clap and cheer. Bruno blushes and scratches his head. Maybe with embarrassment. Maybe because he has lice.

Otto goes next. 'The bear was full after eating the hunter and decided that he needed to lie down for a long nap. But the forest floor was covered in prickly pine cones, so he growled, "I wish I had a bed with five mattresses and six eiderdowns and seven pillows." And—POOF!—the bed appeared in the middle of the forest, big and soft and warm. The bear climbed in and soon he was fast asleep, snoring like a—'

Mia snorts, then settles back into a steady rhythm of snoring.

Otto grins and says, 'The bear was soon snoring like Mia!'

We wait for Josef to choose his wish for the bear. His eyes are closed, scrunched tightly together, and I wonder if he's fallen asleep.

Then, finally, he speaks. 'The next day, the bear went back to his den and he discovered that the Russian soldiers had taken his mama away, so he used his fourth wish. He growled, "I wish my mama would grow wings and fly away from the Russians and fly back home to me, and then I wish—"'

'Hey!' cries Otto. 'Liesl gets to use the fifth wish, not you!'

But Josef doesn't care. His words tumble out, spittle

forming at the corners of his mouth. '"I wish the entire Russian Army would explode into a million tiny pieces that get caught on the wind and blown into the deepest part of the Baltic Sea!"'

We all fall silent.

I cover my face with my hands. Russian soldiers and bombs and disappearing mamas aren't supposed to be here. Not now when we have new friends and fish in our tummies and sunshine on our faces and a game to play.

My eyes fill with hot tears. But before they can spill through my fingers, Karl leaps to his feet and finishes the story with a flourish.

'And of course the wishes came true, because Gustav wasn't only a magic fish but a trustworthy fish who kept his promise. Mama Bear flew back into the den and put on her favorite yellow apron with pink flowers all over and cooked a lovely big supper of roast pork with mashed potatoes and sauerkraut . . . and gherkins. The bear invited all his friends to join them and they ate until they were full and they lived happily ever after.'

'Happily ever after!' cheers Bruno. 'I like that.'

'Me too!' shouts Otto.

'Me too,' whispers Josef.

Me too.

'Come, Josef,' says Bruno when the sun starts to sink in the sky. 'We'd better go.'

Karl steps toward the brothers and I hold my breath, terrified that he's decided to go with them. But he reaches out and shakes Bruno's hand, then Josef's.

'Thank you for the fish,' he says, then steps back closer to Mia, Otto, and me.

He is ours, not theirs.

I hold a German hymnbook out to Josef. 'A gift,' I say. 'A thank-you for sharing your fish.'

Josef stares at the book, then passes it to Bruno.

Bruno flicks through the pages and says, 'Thanks, but . . .'

'It's all right,' I explain, 'we have more copies.'

Bruno laughs. 'But why would we want a hymnbook?'

'To read!' I say.

'I hate reading,' says Bruno.

'Me too,' says Josef.

'Then use the pages to wipe your bottom,' suggests Otto.

Bruno gasps. 'Isn't that a *sin* or something?'

I roll my eyes. 'Shooting people is a sin. Stealing mamas is a sin. Trapping bears is a sin. But wiping your bottom . . . That's just sensible.'

CHAPTER 33

Every day for the next week, we go to the lake. We wait for hours each time, but Bruno and Josef don't come back. We're bitterly disappointed. We pretend it's because we are fond of the brothers. But really it's because we have been dreaming of cooked fish.

'Perhaps they're fishing at another lake,' says Karl.

'Perhaps they got into trouble for going home empty-handed,' I murmur. 'We shouldn't have eaten all their fish.' But in my heart, I know that I'd eat all the fish again if I got the chance.

'Perhaps Josef caught a magic fish called Gustav,' suggests Otto, 'and they've used one of their wishes to find their mama and another wish to fly away to a land of peace and plenty.'

I snort. A land of peace and plenty sounds as fanciful as

a magic fish. Then again, I think I'd rather believe Otto's explanation than mine.

I wipe my nose, pretend the snort was a sneeze, then say, 'Yes, and by now Bruno and Josef have surely used the other three wishes and will be having a *wonderful* time.'

Otto smiles. 'They're playing at the beach!'

'Riding the roller coaster at the fair,' says Karl.

'Eating sausages in buns,' I add.

Mia tugs at my sleeve. 'Mia want sausage,' she whispers. I sigh. We all want sausages.

'Come on,' says Karl.

He lifts Mia onto his shoulders and leads us around the lake in a new direction, to a different farm, where we hope there will be a larder where we'll find sausages . . . or buns . . . or even just a rotten potato.

We crouch behind the woodshed and wait. We are waiting, waiting, watching, and waiting. Waiting makes me tired and hungry. So very, very hungry. Even though I barely move. Because not moving means I can put all my energy into noticing how my tummy groans and complains that it hasn't had anything decent since the fish.

But the waiting pays off because, at last, the farmer goes to the barn and brings out a handcart. He tosses a burlap sack into it and calls to his family. His wife and three girls straggle out of the house, bickering and whining.

If I lived in a house with *my* mama and *my* papa, I

would never behave like that. I would be skipping and laughing and singing and kissing everyone all day long. These girls don't know how lucky they are.

We watch and wait until the family has stumbled down the driveway, into the lane, and away over the hill.

I am about to slip out of hiding when Karl grabs my hand. 'Wait a bit longer,' he says, 'until we make sure there's nobody still in the house.'

I sit back down, but Karl keeps holding my hand.

When we finally sneak inside, the kitchen is bare—not a loaf of bread or a jar of jam or even a blob of suet.

I point to the larder, but the sound of crying makes us all freeze. Even Mia. She hugs Baby to her chest and stares at me, eyes wide.

A girl, about Otto's age, stumbles into the kitchen. She is dirty, with matted hair, but is wearing a pretty yellow dress. She sniffs but doesn't seem bothered that there are four strange children in her home.

'Who are you?' she asks.

'Run!' shouts Otto.

'Wait!' cries the girl. 'Please don't go. There's nobody here but me, and I won't tell.'

I don't run, but I sweep Mia into my arms just in case. 'Where's your family gone?' I ask. 'When will they be back?'

'My family is dead,' says the girl.

'Liar!' shouts Otto. 'We just saw them leaving.'

'They're not my family.' The girl sniffs and wipes her

nose on the hem of the pretty dress. 'This is *my* house, but they are not my family. Papa died in the war. Mama died after the war, and those new people moved in. They stole my home!'

'Russians?' I ask, remembering the wild children who stole our wheelbarrow.

'No,' says the girl. 'East Prussians. Like us. They just arrived one day and told me their home had been burned to the ground, so they were going to live in this one now. I tried to stay, but the mama dragged me out by my hair and told me she'd beat me with the wooden spoon if I ever returned.'

'Then why are you here?' asks Karl.

'I came back to get my things!' She puts her hands on her hips and lifts her chin. 'I watched until they left, then I came in through the front door. I didn't even knock. Because this is *my* house!'

'And because there was nobody at home,' mutters Otto.

He doesn't like the girl. He's already decided.

'I'm taking *my* things,' says the girl, ignoring Otto. She twirls around so the skirt of her dress flies out. 'This is *my* dress. *My* mama sewed it for me. I'm stealing it back because it is *mine*.' She sways from side to side and flutters her eyelashes at Karl.

I look down at my own clothes. They are so tattered and worn, they're barely holding together.

'Are there more clothes?' I ask.

◄◄─►►

When we leave the house, Charlotte comes with us. She is wearing the pretty yellow party dress and carries an onion.

I'm wearing a red-and-white-checked party dress and carry a white cardigan wrapped around six more onions. Otto carries a blanket and four battered tin bowls. Karl carries Mia, who is wearing a pretty white smock. There is nothing else in the house worth stealing.

Charlotte says the people who moved in have been trading everything for food. Even the clothes they will soon need for the winter. I shiver at the thought.

I try to like Charlotte, but I can't. I suppose she might have been nice once upon a time, but it doesn't take long to realize that she is horrible.

I remind myself that Charlotte has lost everything. She doesn't have a kind brother like Otto, or a sweet baby sister like Mia, or a handsome boy like Karl to hug her and hold her hand and make her feel safe. She is not like Bruno and Josef, who have Russian food to fill their bellies and fishing trips to the lake where they can pretend for an hour or two that they are normal children. She has nothing but the yellow party dress her mama sewed.

Before we've even returned to our hut, Charlotte has told Mia that Baby is the ugliest toy she has ever seen. She has laughed at Otto's enormous boots. And she has told me that I stink. I do stink. We all stink. Even Charlotte stinks. But there's no need to say so.

I cook the onions in lots of water. 'Onion soup!' I sing,

and fill the tin bowls to the brim.

I give Mia the cup and pop in most of my share of the onions as well as her own. She's far too thin, and I think she might have stopped growing. It's all right if I never get any bigger, but if Mia stops growing now, she won't even be tall enough to climb into a bed or sit on a normal chair at the dinner table.

'Yum! Yum!' shouts Mia. 'Mia love soup.' She sticks her fingers into the cup and pulls out the pieces of onion, sucking them through her lips as if they're delicate morsels of meat.

My tummy rumbles. I know that my bowl of onion-flavored water won't make a scrap of difference, but Mia is happy for a few moments. That's better than a full tummy any day.

Otto smiles at me. 'Best soup ever, Liesl! Much better than sausages in buns.'

'Lovely dinnerware, too,' says Karl, tapping his fingers against the battered tin bowl.

Charlotte gulps her soup down. She hugs her bowl to her chest and peers at us through narrowed eyes.

'You gave them more than me!' she snarls.

'I didn't,' I say. 'Truly. I measured it out so everyone got the same.'

'Mia has more onion!' whines Charlotte.

'I gave her mine,' I explain.

Mia stops eating and stares.

'It's all right, Mia,' I say. 'Eat up. It's good for you.'

'No!' shouts Charlotte. 'Give it to me!'

She lunges toward Mia, but Otto pushes her aside. Some of his precious soup slops on the ground.

Mia starts crying. I pull her into my lap and feed her bits of onion from my fingers, like a mother bird feeding her chick. I glare at Charlotte.

Charlotte glares back. She scoffs at Otto, who is picking bits of onion off the ground and eating them. She throws the tin bowl at my head and stomps away into the forest.

I hope she never comes back.

Charlotte comes back two days later.

We've had a wonderful start to our day. Otto and Karl caught a squirrel and found three mushrooms. I'm cooking mushroom-and-squirrel casserole, and it smells delicious, even better than onion soup.

Mia is excited because Karl has given her the squirrel tail. It's soft and fluffy, and Mia has decided it's a friend for Baby. She calls it Tail.

'Casserole is ready!' I call out.

Charlotte appears at the edge of the clearing. I think she's been watching, waiting until we have food again.

'Hello!' she sings, as though she is an old friend. As though she didn't try to steal Mia's food. As though she didn't scoff at Otto. As though she didn't throw a bowl at my head.

Otto pulls Mia to his side. Karl takes a step forward so he's half shielding them.

I'm about to tell Charlotte to shoo, but then I see the hollow look in her eyes and the filth on her pretty yellow dress, and I'm filled with pity.

'Hello, Charlotte,' I say. 'Would you like to share our casserole?'

Charlotte nods and sits by the fire. This time she doesn't complain about the taste or the extra bit of squirrel meat I give to Mia. She eats in silence, and when she is done, she whispers, 'Thank you.'

After lunch, I wash the soup pot in the stream, then plonk it down in front of the hut. 'Fräulein Hofmann is waiting!' I call, and Mia, Otto, Karl, and I sit down on the grass, our legs folded.

Charlotte scrunches her nose, uncertain about what is happening, but also sits down. She enjoys our lessons. She sings her twelve times table louder than the rest of us, and reads the story of David and Goliath with wonderful expression.

'Well done, Charlotte,' I say. 'You're a very clever pupil.' Charlotte sits up a little straighter, and for the first time, a smile twitches around the corner of her mouth.

We bathe in the pond, then lie in the grass. I hum a lazy lullaby for Mia, and she dances Baby and Tail across my tummy.

'Look,' says Otto. 'If you stare long enough at the clouds, you can see pictures.'

A new game! A shiver of excitement runs down my spine. I wriggle my back deeper into the grass and stare at the clouds.

'See?' shouts Otto, pointing above the tops of the trees. 'There's a dove!'

We all watch in silence as the fluffy white dove drifts across the sky and turns slowly back into an everyday cloud.

'There's a chair!' cries Karl. 'No, a table! No, a bed.' He tilts his head from side to side, then sighs. 'Oh no, it's just a cloud.'

Otto and I laugh, and Karl joins in.

'I can see a castle,' brags Charlotte.

'Where?' I ask.

'There!' She waves her arm all about. 'It has five towers and a drawbridge, and a moat filled with crocodiles.'

'You can't see all that,' Otto scoffs.

'Can too!' shouts Charlotte. 'I can't help it if I'm better at seeing cloud pictures than the rest of you.'

She flutters her eyelashes at Karl, but he's too busy looking for cloud tables and cloud chairs and cloud beds to notice.

'Look! Look!' Mia jumps up and points at the sky. 'Mia see cow. Woof! Woof!'

Charlotte snorts. 'That baby is *so* dumb!'

'Take that back!' shouts Otto.

'I can't,' Charlotte sneers. 'I've already said it. Besides, it's true. She's the dumbest baby in the world.' Then she turns to me. 'When's supper?'

I grit my teeth and shrug.

'What sort of family is this?' screams Charlotte.

She leaps to her feet, kicks me in the knee, and runs away into the forest once more.

'Good riddance,' says Otto.

CHAPTER 34

I hold Mia on my hip and point at the photo on the wall of our hut. 'Mama,' I say, and wait for Mia to say it. Instead, she clutches Baby and Tail to her chest and buries her face in their fur.

'That's Mama,' I repeat. 'You know Mama. Mama loves Mia and Otto and Liesl. Mama is the most beautiful woman in the world.'

I want to say that soon Mama will find us and we'll live happily ever after, but the words won't come out.

Instead I beg, 'Please, Mia, say *Mama*.'

Mia drops Tail and concentrates on rubbing her chin against Baby.

I point to Papa in the photo and say, 'Papa.'

Mia flops her head onto my shoulder and refuses to speak. She is too hungry. Too tired. Too weak.

Summer has gone and so have its berries and wild sorrel, its squirrels and chicks, its bugs and tadpoles and frogs. East Prussia is chill and stark and growing leaner by the day. It's getting harder and harder to find something to eat. We've been living off weeds and water.

Even the people who live in the villages and on the farms can be seen straggling across the meadows, searching desperately for a mushroom, a potato, a stalk of wheat that has lain unnoticed. If the world were a larder, East Prussia would be the top shelf where all the empty jars are stored.

I carry Mia out into the sunshine. Otto and Karl are mending my boots. Otto is using a rock and some rusty old nails to hammer the sole back onto my brown boot. Karl is using his knife and some squirrel skin to patch the hole in the toe of my black boot. Soon my boots will be as good as new . . . or, at least, watertight and warm. And even more unusual than when Opa first made them.

The thought of Opa makes my eyes prickle.

Karl nods at me. Otto holds up my brown boot, its sole now nailed on like a board over a broken window. I smile. But none of us speak. We are all too hungry. Too tired.

I sit with Mia and watch as Otto sorts the leftover nails and Karl sharpens his knife. The only sound is the swoosh of metal on rock and the flutter of birds gathering, preparing to fly south for the winter.

Suddenly, Mia squeals. She claps her hands and cries, 'Woof! Woof!'

'It's all right, Mia,' I coo, rocking her from side to side.

But she claps again and wriggles and shouts, 'Woof! Woof!'

My neck prickles. Is Mia so starving that she's gone mad? 'Shhh, shhh,' I say, trying to soothe her, but she jumps out of my lap and runs away, barking like a rabid dog.

I run after her, but I have only gone a few yards when I stop and squeal. Just like Mia! And then I clap and cheer.

For walking out of the forest and into the clearing are Bruno and Josef. And tagging along behind them is a big, fat, cream-colored cow.

At first, I think it's a mirage. That I, too, am going mad with hunger. But still I can't stop cheering.

Then Bruno waves and Josef sings, 'Helloooo, Liesl! We've brought you a present!'

And the cow bellows and tosses her head, and I know, I know, I know that they are real!

They walk toward us, the cow's udder swaying from side to side, heavy with milk.

Mia squeals. 'Mia love cow! Woof! Woof!'

And I sing, 'Liesl love cow too! Woof! Woof!'

I sit on the upturned soup pot and milk the cow into our bucket. As I roll my fingers down her soft pink teats, I say a silent thank-you to Dmitri for teaching me how to milk, and an out-loud thank-you to Bruno and Josef for bringing such a wonderful gift. A dairy cow is even better than a fishing rod.

Otto, Mia, Bruno, Josef, and Karl hover. I milk some, pour it into cups and bowls, we gulp it down, and then I milk some more. I milk until the cow is dry and our tummies are bulging.

Bruno tethers the cow to a small log so she can move around easily but can't gallop away. She chomps on the grass, drinks from the stream, chews her cud, licks her nose, and blinks. She is the most beautiful thing I have ever seen. A giant lump of gold. Pure treasure. Because later in the day, I will milk her again and we will drink until we are full. And in the morning, we can do it all over again.

'Can you stay for a while?' I ask Bruno and Josef. 'Before you have to go home.'

'We're not going home,' says Bruno.

'We have no home,' says Josef.

'The Russians headed east with another herd of cows just yesterday,' Bruno explains. 'They made us go along to help.'

'We didn't want to go to Russia,' says Josef. 'It's a long way, you know!'

Bruno nods. 'So when one of the cows ran away from the herd, we said we'd catch it and bring it back. But by the time we caught her, we were out of sight, so we just kept running!'

'Good idea!' cheers Karl.

'And the cow was glad to come with us,' says Josef. 'She keeps licking our ears and necks as though she wants to thank us for saving her from the Russians.'

'I would lick your ears and neck too,' says Otto, 'if you'd saved me from the Russians.'

We all burst out laughing. It's easy to talk and laugh now that we have food in our bellies.

'Anyway,' says Bruno, 'we can't go home, because the soldiers who are still there will know we've run away. They'll probably hit us, or send us back east . . . or both.'

'*And* they'll take the cow from us,' adds Josef.

'What's her name?' asks Otto.

Josef shrugs.

'Such a beautiful cow needs a name,' I say. 'A really special name.'

'Daisy?' suggests Josef.

'Buttercup,' says Karl.

'Gustav!' shouts Bruno. He really did love the story of Gustav the magic fish.

'Cows are *girls*,' I explain.

Bruno blushes. 'I forgot.'

'Yummy!' yells Mia.

I remind her that yummy is what we say when we drink the cow's milk. But Mia insists and sings, 'Yummy! Yummy!'

So the cow is given her special name: Yummy Cow.

Yummy Cow is magic. She has only been here for a week and already she has changed our lives.

Mia, who had become so thin and quiet and listless, is walking through the grass, singing a little song. She reaches Yummy Cow, leans forward, and kisses the pink slimy nose. Yummy Cow blinks, moos, and licks Mia's neck. Mia squeals and runs around, waving her arms in the air. She is cute and funny and full of life once more.

Otto, Karl, Bruno, and Josef are playing a game. A real run-about game! Karl has a bandage wrapped around his eyes and is staggering, grabbing, lunging, laughing. Otto, Bruno, and Josef snicker and rustle through the grass, dodging from his grasp at the last possible moment. Karl dives, collides with Bruno, and sends them both tumbling into a bush. They sit up, howling with laughter.

Karl pulls the bandages off his eyes and waves at me. His eyes are no longer dull and dark, but shine a deep rich green. Like emeralds. Like Christmas trees.

Mia runs toward me and throws herself into my lap. Yummy Cow is right at her heels. The cow stands in front of me, lifts her head, and bellows, ready for her evening milking. Mia buries her head in my chest and squeals, 'Yummy Cow bite. Help! Help!' But she is giggling, and I know that she is simply playing with her new friend.

The boys move on to a strange new game they've invented that seems to be a mix of leapfrog, tag, and wrestling.

I sit on the upturned soup pot and milk Yummy Cow. Mia stands at the cow's head, patting the tuft of hair between her horns and singing nursery rhymes. I press into Yummy Cow's fat, warm side and sing along with Mia, milking to the rhythm of our tune. I am filled with a sense of happiness and peace.

That night, the sky is clear and the air is frosty. I am

wondering how we will keep warm, when Yummy Cow comes crashing into the hut. She stands patiently while we wriggle about, making a space for her in our midst, then plops to the floor.

Mia snuggles into the cow's warm, soft belly and falls asleep. Soon she is snoring.

Otto shrugs, then presses in against the cow, and we all do the same.

Yummy Cow is as good as five mattresses and six eiderdowns and a big log fire.

Magic.

CHAPTER 35

Three days later, Charlotte returns. The boys are over at the pond, bathing, splashing, laughing, draping pond scum over their heads like wigs. Mia is playing with Baby and Tail, tucking them into their Russian helmet bed, singing them a lullaby. I am milking Yummy Cow, and the bucket is half full with frothy, creamy milk.

Charlotte walks silently across the clearing and is peering over my shoulder into the bucket before I know she's there.

'Yum!' she gasps.

I dip the cup into the bucket, fill it with milk, and pass it to her. She gulps it so fast that milk dribbles from the corners of her mouth and down her chest. I refill the cup, and this time she manages to get it all down her throat.

After the third cup, the wild animal look is gone from her

eyes and she sits on the ground at my side while I finish the milking. Her hair is putrid with mud, her dress is torn, and she has deep cuts on both her legs.

'What happened?' I ask.

'I tried to get on a train to Lithuania, but I fell off.' She licks her milky lips. 'There's bread in Lithuania.'

Bread! My mouth waters at the thought. Even though we've had full bellies every day since Yummy Cow arrived, the thought of bread drives me crazy. I can't remember when I last ate a slice of bread, or even a *crust* of bread. I'd pay a million Reichsmark for just one tiny, stale crust of bread.

Oma's words to Mama pop into my mind: 'A mere scrap of bread will cost a diamond.' It sounded so silly at the time. But now I understand.

'Really?' I ask. '*Proper* bread?'

Charlotte nods. 'And corn and ham. *Everybody* is jumping on the trains to Lithuania. But it's tricky because you have to get on while they're moving. And you have to ride in the freight cars, or hang off the sides, or balance on the roof. You can't just climb aboard like a proper passenger. Unless you have a ticket and a travel pass. Which I don't. You have to be rich to get a ticket and a pass. Or important. Or bribe a guard . . . with jewelry or money . . . or a cow.'

I laugh. 'I don't think a guard would accept a cow as a bribe. A guard can slip jewelry or money into his pocket without being seen, but people would notice a cow.'

Charlotte shrugs. 'You could try,' she says.

The next morning, Charlotte is gone. And so is Yummy Cow.

'Maybe Charlotte took Yummy Cow for a walk,' says Bruno.

'Maybe Yummy Cow ran away and Charlotte has gone to find her,' says Josef.

But Karl, Otto, and I know what Charlotte is like. Charlotte doesn't do anything for anyone other than herself.

'Charlotte is gone,' I say. 'Yummy Cow is gone.'

Mia drops to the ground and weeps softly into the dirt. But later in the day, Charlotte returns.

'Look!' cries Bruno. He leaps to his feet and runs toward her.

We all follow, laughing, waving, peering into the forest, each wanting to be the first to spot Yummy Cow crashing through the trees.

But Yummy Cow isn't there.

Charlotte skips into our midst and does a pirouette. 'Well?' she sings. 'Do you like it?'

She is wearing a new dress. It's pink with tiny white flowers and puffy sleeves.

Charlotte has swapped Yummy Cow for a dress!

She hasn't used our beautiful, precious cow to bribe a guard and get to Lithuania. She hasn't swapped her for food that she can share with the rest of us. All she has gained is a dress. It's not even a winter dress. It's a stupid summer dress that will barely keep her warm enough in the middle of the day now that autumn is here.

'What have you done?' I scream. 'You stupid, selfish, annoying little rat! What have you done?'

I rush at Charlotte and knock her to the ground. I slap her across the cheek, and then I ball my hand into a fist and pull it up into the air because I'm going to punch her in the nose. Really hard. Over and over again.

But Mia squeaks, and I look up, and she and Otto are staring at me, their eyes wide with horror. Otto's hands fly to his head, where they clutch at his dirty hair. Mia's bottom lip is sticking out and wobbling. They do not like this crazy new sister.

I lower my fist, stand, and stomp away into the forest. When I return, Charlotte is crying.

Good! I think. *She deserves to be filled with shame and remorse.*

But when I sit beside her, she whines, 'Nobody told me I look pretty in my new dress. Not even Karl.'

I clench my jaw so tightly that my teeth squeak. I want to tell her that she has been a wicked girl. I want to explain that Yummy Cow was the only thing that was keeping us fed. I want to shout that because of her stupid, selfish actions, we will all go to bed hungry tonight, and we will wake up even hungrier in the morning, and then we will all starve.

But I don't. What's the use? No amount of screaming or punching will bring Yummy Cow back to us.

Charlotte whimpers. I sigh. I reach out and touch her puffy sleeve.

'That is a beautiful dress, Charlotte,' I whisper. 'And you look very, *very* pretty.'

Charlotte stares at me, mouth gaping, and then she smiles. It is a lovely smile, and I think I catch a glimpse of the sweet little girl she used to be. Before she lost her mama and her papa. Before she became a wild child. Before starving for food and love made her mean.

I wrap my arm around her shoulder, and she presses into me.

'And now,' she says, 'you probably should apologize for pushing me over and slapping me.'

That night, we lie in the dark and talk about what to do. Except for Mia. She cries softly in my arms, and she coughs. The shock of losing Yummy Cow has made her sick.

'We can't stay here,' says Bruno.

'But it's safe here,' I whisper.

'There's nothing safe about starving,' he says. He's right, of course.

'But where would we go?' asks Karl.

'That's obvious!' cries Charlotte. She waits for us to ask, but nobody wants to talk to her. Finally, she shouts, 'Lithuania!'

Charlotte tells us all the stories she has heard about Lithuania. 'They have bread. Lots of bread. And vegetables and salted ham and *more* bread with butter.'

We are silent, except for the rumbling of tummies.

We're thinking about the Lithuanian food. Especially the Lithuanian bread.

'You have to beg,' says Charlotte, 'but still . . .'

'We could steal it,' says Josef.

'Stealing is wrong!' snaps Charlotte.

I roll my eyes, but nobody can see it in the dark.

'Of course, there are *witches* in Lithuania,' says Charlotte, her voice full of knowing. 'Mean, bony witches who like to eat children. They live in the forests and lurk around the edges of the villages, hoping to catch little ones who wander off alone.'

'Shhh!' I hiss. 'You'll scare Mia.'

'Mia's too dumb to understand,' says Charlotte. 'Anyway, if you're going to Lithuania, you really should be prepared for the witches. So Mia doesn't get caught and eaten.'

'There are no witches!' I shout, but a shiver runs down my spine.

'Josef and I know which trains go to Lithuania,' says Bruno. 'We've been to the station with the Russian soldiers.' The station is in a village not far from here. Some trains pass straight through, but others stop for passengers or for freight.

'So we can jump aboard,' says Otto. 'Easy.'

'Not if the guards spot you!' cries Charlotte. 'I've seen them throw people off the train, even when it's moving.'

'Not children!' I gasp.

But the second the words are out, I wonder why I bothered. I've seen much worse.

We all have.

<del>←←→→</del>

We bundle up our blankets, bowls, cups, spoons, and Tail the squirrel tail. I pull our two family photos down from the wall and stuff them deep into my underwear. I dress Mia in her winter coat, both grateful and terrified that it still fits her, and press Baby to her chest.

'What about Mama?' asks Otto.

I'm about to say that it doesn't matter. That Mama will never find us now. But I cannot say such a thing to Otto. I cannot say such a thing to myself.

'We could leave her a note,' I suggest. 'I'll write a message in the hymnbook with charcoal and leave it in the hut.'

Otto smiles. 'Good idea.'

I write: *Dear Mama, We are in Lithuania. From Liesl Anna Wolf, Otto Friedrich Wolf, and Mia Hilda Wolf.*

I apologize to Otto. 'It's not much, but writing with charcoal is messy, and I can only use the blank spaces at the edge of the pages, and the letters have to be really big or you can't read them.'

'It'll do,' says Otto, and he hugs me.

Bruno and Josef guide us through the forest, across meadows, along sheltered country roads, until we reach the train station. We hide in the trees and watch, all afternoon and into the night, until the train to Lithuania arrives.

We creep past the station, past the lights, and wait by the tracks in the moonlight.

Karl makes a sling from a blanket and straps Mia to my

back. He wedges Baby down in the sling for safekeeping. He will jump on the train first, then pull me up. Otto, Charlotte, Bruno, and Josef must look after themselves.

The whistle blows.

The train chugs out of the station toward us. My heart thumps in my chest, harder and faster. The train picks up speed.

'It's going too fast!' I gasp.

'No, it's not!' shouts Karl. 'You're brave and strong, Liesl. We can do this together.'

He grabs my shoulders, leans forward, and kisses me. On the lips!

I gasp. And then I smile. Charlotte frowns.

The engine passes and we dash up to the track. The freight wagons rattle by, faster and faster. Bruno runs and jumps and swings himself aboard. Josef and Otto follow. Charlotte tries and slips, but Karl grabs her and tosses her into a wagon, then pulls himself aboard too.

'Liesl!' he shouts. 'Run! Run!'

And I do run, but as I reach for the edge of the wagon, Charlotte throws a chunk of coal at me and I trip. I trip and tumble into a ditch, and when I look up again, the last wagon is disappearing around a curve in the track.

CHAPTER 36

The train is gone, and everyone is gone with it.

Charlotte.

Josef.

Bruno.

Karl.

I sob. Otto!

The train is gone, and it won't stop until it gets to Lithuania. I have lost Otto. I promised Mama that I would keep him safe, and now I have lost him.

Mia is crying, and I'm crying too. I untie the blanket and pull her into my lap. I sit in the grass, in the dark, rocking back and forth, howling.

I've lost Otto, and I don't know how I will ever find him again. I cannot stay here, but I cannot catch the train without Karl's help. Mia is too heavy and too little, both at the same time.

'I've lost Otto,' I cry. 'I'm sorry, Mia. I'm sorry!'

Mia screams, 'Otto! Otto! Mia want Otto!'

But I can't give her Otto. How will Mia and I survive without him?

I cry and cry, until a voice shouts through the dark. 'Liesl! Mia!'

I jump to my feet, swing Mia into my arms, and run along the track. I stumble, but keep running and crying and shouting until we collide with the boy who is limping and crying and cursing Hitler and Winston Churchill and Franklin Roosevelt and Gustave Eiffel.

Otto has jumped off the speeding train and run back to me!

'You stupid boy!' I shout. 'You could have been killed!'

'You stupid girl!' he shouts. 'Why didn't you get on the train?'

'Stupid! Stupid!' shouts Mia, and she punches me in the chest.

I laugh. I cry. I hug Otto and Mia.

I squeeze them until Mia squeals, 'Ouch! Too much love.'

But there is no such thing as too much love. I hug them on and on and on, until Mia wriggles and squirms so hard that I stumble.

I fall to the ground, and something sharp sticks into my leg. I try to pull it away but realize that it's poking from inside my coat. Inside the lining.

I pull my coat off and rip the lining along the seam. A gold bracelet, a ruby brooch, a sapphire ring, and a pair of pearl earrings fall onto the dirt and glisten in the moonlight.

'Jewels!' says Otto.

'Pretty,' coos Mia.

'Bribes!' I cry.

The next night, we travel by train as third-class passengers. The guard lets us aboard for a ruby brooch, a pair of pearl earrings, and our one extra blanket. He snatches Baby, too, but Mia screams so loudly that he gives the ugly toy straight back.

We have to sit on the floor, tucked between the seats, but we don't care. This is the best shelter we've had in months, and we feel like a little prince and princesses traveling in the royal carriage. We're on our way to Lithuania.

'Why is everyone staring at us?' asks Otto.

'They're jealous of my boots,' I say, and wriggle my feet to show off the brown boot with the rusty nails sticking out around the edges and the black boot with the squirrel fur poking out through the hole in the toe. 'Everyone is wishing they had a fine pair of boots just like mine.'

We giggle.

The lady sitting closest to us holds her handkerchief over her nose and sniffs.

We giggle again, but I feel my cheeks burn too.

A new guard walks into the train car. He spots Otto, Mia, and me and storms down the aisle. I take a deep breath, reach into my pocket, and grab the gold bracelet. I hold it up and smile. The guard snorts, slips the bracelet into his own pocket, and walks away. So easy!

'Thank you, Mama,' I whisper. Otto wriggles about on the floor. 'What are you doing?' I ask.

'I'm trying to feel with my bottom,' he says.

'Feel what?'

'How much jewelry Mama has sewn into the lining of my coat.'

'Mama sewed jewelry into *your* coat too?' I gasp.

'And Mia's,' he says.

I grin.

Mia snores, her head in my lap. Her chest rattles and wheezes a little between the snorts.

Otto grows sleepy. 'Tell me about Lithuania, Liesl,' he murmurs.

'There's bread,' I say. 'Lots of bread.'

'And butter,' he slurs.

'And maybe even jam.' My mouth waters at the thought of apricots and sugar dancing across my tongue.

Otto slumps into my side, fast asleep already. But I go on, painting the picture of Lithuania in my mind.

By the time we cross the border, Lithuania has grown into a fairy-tale land of plenty where we will live in a house made from almond cake, sleep in beds of soft white bread, bathe in tubs of milk, and eat chocolate and marzipan three times a day. It's almost as good as the Germany I once imagined after the war.

Except that no matter how hard I try, I can't find Mama.

Not even here, in my daydreams.

The guard nudges me with his boot. 'Off you get now. Before the station. Unless you want to get caught by the Russians and sent back to where you came from. Or sent somewhere worse.'

He hustles us toward the door at the back of the train car and opens it. Mia coughs as the cold air hits her little body. The train is slowing down, but it still doesn't look safe to jump.

'Get off,' growls the guard.

'Thank you,' I say.

It's a stupid thing to say to someone who's getting ready to push you off a moving train even though you've paid him enough rubies and pearls for a *hundred* tickets, but I'm truly grateful that we've made it to Lithuania.

I hoist Mia onto my hip, grab Otto by the hand, and jump. Lithuania knocks the wind out of me. It cuts Mia's forehead, skins Otto's nose and chin, and snaps off three of Baby's legs.

But we don't care. We've made it. We are here in the land of plenty.

VANISHING WOLVES

CHAPTER 37

This one,' says Otto, pointing to a house.

We have passed other houses, but there were snarling dogs and scowling farmers and hand-painted signs on gates that might have said *No begging*, or *We hate dirty Germans*. Then again, they might also have said *Bread for sale*, or *Get your free chocolate here*. We don't know because we don't read Lithuanian.

This house sits at the edge of a village. It's small, low, and dark, the timber unpainted, maybe even rotting. The picket fence has slats missing, and the garden looks like it's been dug up by a plague of moles or a very hungry pig searching for a turnip. This is not a wealthy home. But there are lace curtains in the two tiny windows, a cheerful blue door, and smoke billowing from the chimney.

We stare at the house.

'Together or just me?' asks Otto.

'Three of us all begging at once might scare whoever comes to the door,' I say. 'Then again, if you're alone, they might grab you or hit you.'

Mia whimpers at the mention of hitting, and Otto's eyes widen.

'Together,' I say.

We open the gate and walk up the path. My knees shake, from hunger, but fear, too. We're used to stealing, hunting, scavenging, but not begging.

Otto knocks on the front door, then steps back. We wait. Nobody answers.

Otto knocks again.

A voice calls from somewhere out the back. An old man hobbles around the side of the house. He is dressed in muddy trousers and a coarse cloth shirt. Gray hair sticks out from beneath a black cap, and he has a pitchfork over his shoulder. I flinch at the sight of the pitchfork. Metal prongs would hurt much more than dog teeth.

'Good day,' I squeak. I bite my lip, unsure of what to say next.

'We're hungry!' shouts Otto. Mia coughs.

The old man grumbles and leans the pitchfork against the wall. He opens the front door and shouts something in Lithuanian. An old woman appears. She is wearing a black dress, a tattered brown apron, and a matching brown scarf around her head.

She stares at Otto and me, but when she notices Mia, her face breaks into a smile. The smile is full of crooked teeth, but it sets her eyes sparkling and her hands reaching forward. She drags me in through the door and pulls Mia from my back and into her arms.

The old man shoves Otto after me, and before we know what has happened, we are seated at a rough wooden table with three bowls of soup. We gobble greedily, and then, like a miracle, three pieces of bread and butter replace our empty bowls. We eat in silence, savoring every mouthful.

The old woman frowns at the rattle in Mia's chest. She pulls a jar of ointment down from the top of a cupboard and rubs it onto Mia's back. It smells like cloves and cinnamon, and Mia loves it. She smiles and closes her eyes and murmurs. The old man and the old woman don't speak German, and they don't speak Mia, but they understand. The old man chuckles, and the old woman kisses Mia on the head. She grimaces a bit at the smell, but kisses Mia again and again. Soup, bread, butter, medicine, kindness, and kisses.

Lithuania really is a land of plenty!

Otto and I spend the afternoon helping the old man in the garden. There's no plague of moles or turnip-snuffling pig. Just a crop of potatoes that needs to be dug up before winter arrives and freezes the soil.

The old woman sits in a chair at the back of the house, wiping the mud off the potatoes. Mia sits at her side, playing a game where she puts a potato in a bucket, claps her hands, then takes the potato out again. The woman watches and laughs as though this is the cleverest thing she has ever seen.

When the sun sets, the old woman shoos us toward a tap. We must wash off all the mud before we're allowed inside.

The water is so cold it hurts, but it's worth it, because after our hands and faces are inspected, we are seated at the kitchen table once more and each fed a bowl of thick, warm cornmeal. The old couple don't eat, and I realize they have given all their food to us.

'Thank you,' I say over and over again between mouthfuls.

'Me too,' says Otto.

'Mia love corn. Yum! Yum!' sings Mia. She loves it so much that she doesn't rub any in her hair but gobbles it all up. Otto and I do the dishes while the old woman cuddles Mia and rubs the clove-and-cinnamon ointment into her chest and back once more. Then the old man takes us out to a wonky shed that is filled with chickens. He scatters straw on the floor and points. Otto, Mia, and I stare at him, not understanding.

'Perhaps he wants us to make nests for the chickens,' says Otto. 'Maybe Lithuanian chickens aren't very smart and don't know how to do it on their own.'

Mia grabs a handful of straw, sits it on her head, and rubs it into her knotted hair.

I shrug. A shrug means the same thing in all languages.

The old man presses his hands together and pretends they're a pillow. He closes his eyes and snores. This is our bed for the night.

'Thank you,' I say again, grateful for a safe, dry place to sleep. 'Thank you.'

'Me too,' whispers Otto.

'Mia too,' says Mia.

We snuggle into the straw and I sing Mia a lullaby, the one about ducklings and doves, chickens and goslings. She sings along and makes sweet little beak actions with both hands, pecking my cheeks and ears and nose.

When we are done, a chicken flaps down from her roost and settles on my leg.

'Oh look, Mia,' I say. 'The chicken liked our song.'

Mia stares at the chicken, then squeals, 'Mia love chicken. Yum! Yum!'

The chicken ruffles her feathers as though offended.

'Woof! Woof!' shouts Mia.

Otto and I giggle and Mia gurgles along.

It's so easy to giggle when your tummy's full and there's a real oma and opa just a short skip away.

The old man wakes us in the morning with a smile and a small cotton bag. The bag contains a chunk of bread and a handful of cornmeal. We are being sent on our way.

The old woman stands at the gate to wave us off, but before we go she draws a cross with her wrinkled finger on each of our foreheads. She is blessing us!

The old couple cannot let us stay. Perhaps they are too poor. Or perhaps they are worried that Mia will eat their chickens. But they have given us full tummies, a good night's sleep, a blessing, a few hours of happiness, and hope. 'Thank you,' I say again, even though it's not enough.

And then I remember Mama's jewels.

I hold out the sapphire ring for the old woman, but she shakes her head and closes my hand back around it.

I will never forget their kindness.

CHAPTER 38

The village is poor but pretty. There are more dark timber homes like the one we've just left, but others are painted—egg-yolk yellow, some with red window frames or green shutters. The paint is always thin, always peeling. It can't be any other way after a war. But the color survives, bright and cheerful.

Broken picket fences surround weed-filled gardens, but the trees are clinging to their last autumn leaves, and a matching carpet spreads out from their trunks—red, orange, yellow. More color. More light between the branches.

We see a woman working in her garden; another carrying a bundle of sticks along the street; a man leading a pig down a lane; more women standing in doorways. Nobody smiles or waves or says hello, but they nod to show that they have seen us. And they don't curse or yell or throw rocks at our heads or chase us away with brooms.

They don't even mind when we sit by a well and eat our food. The bread is stale but delicious. The cornmeal is hard to eat, but we wash it down with mouthfuls of water from the pump. Our bellies are full once more.

'I like Lithuania,' whispers Otto.

'Me too,' I say.

Mia picks a crumb from the dirt and pops it into her mouth. She grins.

'This is a kind village,' I say. 'I think it's a good place to ask for more food. Maybe even a place to stay.'

'Shouldn't we look for Karl?' asks Otto. 'And Josef and Bruno?' He doesn't mention Charlotte.

I bite my lip. Where would we begin? We don't know how far they traveled before they jumped off the train. We have no idea where they might be, which makes finding them about as likely as finding a needle in a haystack. I don't want to think about it, but now Otto has made me.

I remember Karl's kiss just moments before I last saw him. I bite my lip so hard it hurts. My chest hurts too. *Karl is lost,* I think. *Like Mama.*

I take a deep breath and force a smile onto my face. 'Food first, then we can worry about Karl.'

'And Josef and Bruno,' adds Otto.

'Yummy Cow,' says Mia.

I sigh. How many lies can I tell before I lose track of what is true and what is make-believe?

I bend down and smile at Mia. 'Yummy Cow has gone

back to her mama,' I say. 'We might not see her for a little while.'

Mia's bottom lip wobbles, and she clutches Baby more tightly.

'But now,' I announce, forcing my voice to sound cheerful, 'it's time to gather some food.'

I wave the cotton bag in the air and turn around and around. I stop and point at the prettiest house I see. It is yellow, and the fence has no missing pickets.

I make Otto and Mia wait by the well while I cross the road, open the gate, and knock at the door. A woman answers. She wears a flowery apron and a red scarf around her hair. Her face is gray and thin, but her eyes are bright.

She looks past me, up and down the street, then nods.

She disappears inside and returns with a slice of bread. I pop it into the cotton bag and say, 'Thank you.'

The door closes. No smile. No farewell. But bread. And she didn't even ask for payment.

I run back to Mia and Otto, waving the bag like a victory flag.

They clap and cheer, and Mia presses Baby to my cheek, saying, 'Kiss for Liesl.'

'I'll try the next house,' says Otto.

I keep the bag with the bread. We don't want people to think we're being greedy.

Otto knocks and smiles and holds out his hands. This housewife returns with an egg. A beautiful fresh egg! But when Otto tries to take it, she pulls it away and yells at him in Lithuanian. Otto runs back to me, frowning, confused.

'I suppose she wants us to pay,' I say.

Otto wriggles out of his coat and we rip the seam apart. A little pile of bracelets and earrings falls, out onto the ground. Mama's bracelets and earrings. I pick through them all, trying to work out how much an egg is worth, and settle on a fine silver bracelet with a tiny silver heart hanging from the catch.

Otto runs back to the house and knocks on the door. The woman reappears, scowling, but holding the egg in her hand. They swap, silver for food, and the woman slams the door in Otto's face.

We go from door to door, begging and receiving— another slice of bread, a tiny pat of butter wrapped in a scrap of cloth, a handful of flour, a potato. A little here, a little there. Sometimes it is given. Sometimes we pay. But we don't mind, because all the little bits add up to plenty. Our cotton sack is fat and full. Tonight, our bellies will be fat and full.

We have passed through the village and there is just one house left. Perhaps here we can ask for a place to sleep—a chicken coop or a woodshed. Maybe even a rug in front of the fireplace. After all, this is Lithuania, land of plenty.

I step up to the front door and knock. I hear voices from inside, and my heart leaps for joy. This is going to be a kind house. I just know it. I start to dream of ham and potatoes and bread and butter and even a real bed. I imagine pillows and eiderdowns and—

The door opens and out flies a dog. I stumble backward and fall onto my bottom. I am frozen with fear, which, thankfully, seems to confuse the dog. He stands before me, big and black, feet wide apart, hackles raised around his neck like a lion's mane. He snarls, pulling back his lips to reveal two perfect rows of sharp white teeth, including two enormous fangs.

A man peers from the window, laughing. All *his* teeth are missing, rotten to the roots.

The dog snarls again and scrapes at the ground with his back paws.

'Run, Liesl! Run!' shouts Otto.

'No, you run first!' I cry. 'Get Mia away from here!'

I wait until they have scuttled down the road, then jump to my feet. The dog leaps at me and sinks his teeth into my hand. I scream, pull free, and slam the gate in the dog's face. The dog throws himself at the fence, growling and frothing at the mouth. He can't get out, but I sprint like a hare, just in case.

I catch up to Mia and Otto, and we run out of the village, across the meadows, through swampy flats, and into a forest. At last we stop. My hand is throbbing and bleeding, and I realize that the bag full of food has been dropped somewhere along the way.

Mia is screaming, coughing, stamping her feet in a tantrum of fear.

Otto is shouting, 'Hitler is a pig and a rat and a worm in the dirt, and even though he's dead, I still hate him because he is still ruining our lives. I hate him! I hate him! I hate him! And I hate Lithuania, too!'

I look around at the dark, thick forest. My head spins and my heart thumps and my legs shake.

'I hate Lithuania! I hate it!' shouts Otto. And right now, I do too.

I am covered in a white blanket. How strange it seems. I thought we had fallen asleep in a forest, huddled in our coats, tucked between the roots of a giant oak tree, hoping we were hidden from rabid dogs. But this morning, I am covered in a white blanket.

I try to force myself awake, but I don't want to because, right now, I am a princess and I'm lying in a beautiful room where everything is white—white walls, white carpet, a white four-poster bed with a soft white eiderdown. The white door opens and a mama, dressed all in white, floats in, carrying a glass of milk and soft, freshly baked white bread rolls. I smile at the mama, but inside I feel a twinge of panic. She is pretty and has a soft, kind face, but she is not *my* mama. I know I should be grateful for the beautiful room and the warm bed and the delicious breakfast and the real live mama who is taking care of me. I know that *any* mama is better than no mama. But this is not my mama, and my smile slips away, and a tear dribbles down my cheek.

'Liesl!' cries Otto. 'Wake up!'

I open my eyes and the white room is still here. But this

one is made of snow, a blanket of white snow, and it's icy, and there is no kind and caring mama.

'Liesl!' shouts Otto. 'I can't wake Mia. She's so cold and I can't get her to open her eyes and I'm scared.'

I sit up, now fully awake. I feel ice in my hands and feet and cheeks and nose. I feel the ache of muscles and bones that have grown too cold overnight. And I see fear in Otto's face. He's shaking Mia, but her little eyes stay closed.

I think of Mia the day we left our home in the blizzard and how silent she became as her little body froze. I think of Oma the day we said farewell and how she didn't wake up, even when we kissed her. I remember Charlotte's warning that there are witches in Lithuania, and I think of all the stories I have read about witches who put curses on little girls that make them fall asleep and never open their eyes again. And then I panic.

'Mia!' I shout. 'Wake up! Wake up!'

I rub her arms and legs. I rub her little chest. I shake her gently, then not so gently. I lift her into my arms and rub her back. I rub and pat and shake and rub and, at last, she coughs.

She coughs and her whole body shakes, and her chest sounds like there's a brook babbling through it.

I lie her back in my arms and whisper, 'Mia, say good morning to Baby.'

I press Baby to her body, but she doesn't wrap her arms around the ugly rabbit or even open her eyes. And her lips are the wrong color. Lips aren't meant to be blue.

I quickly brush the snow and leaves off our bodies and

stand, pressing Mia to my chest. I turn around, looking between the trees. As though I will find something helpful—a warm cottage, a mama, a papa, an opa, a doctor, a cow who will huddle up to Mia and warm her blood once more.

'We need help!' I scream.

But the second the words are out of my mouth, I realize how stupid they are. Of *course* we need help. We are children. We've needed help from the moment we lost Mama, but we haven't been able to find it. Not proper, lasting help.

I stare at Mia's blue lips. Now is *not* the time to give up. 'Come on,' I say to Otto.

We rush and stumble out of the forest, across a snowy field, and head toward the first farm we see. The buildings are dark and low—a house, a shed, and a barn. They are iced with snow, but there is smoke coming out of the chimney, and a light shines in one of the windows.

Mia is lifeless in my arms. I shake her, but she doesn't even flinch. I rush toward the house.

'What if there's a dog?' asks Otto.

I look down at Mia. I can't outrun a dog with my baby sister in my arms.

'I'll go first,' says Otto. 'Just in case.'

He stomps through the snow and mud in his big Russian boots, trying to look brave. Instead he looks small and scared. He hesitates at the door, but when he glances back and sees Mia like a floppy rag doll in my arms, he squares his shoulders and knocks.

The door opens, and a stocky man with one arm steps out. He sees Otto and looks up and down the road. Otto points to me and says something. The man frowns but doesn't move, so Otto grabs him by his empty sleeve and drags him across the snow to where I am standing.

The man sees Mia and his hand shoots up to his head. His face is filled with pain. 'Come! Come!' he says in German. 'Quickly. Inside.'

I follow him across the snow and step over the threshold into a warm, dry room with a blazing fire and—I sob at the sight—a mama with outstretched arms.

CHAPTER 39

Magdalena and Dovydas are kind and gentle and both speak German. Before the war, Magdalena was a schoolteacher, but the Germans took the Jewish headmaster away and burned the school down. Before the war, they had a little girl called Daina, but she grew ill and there was no doctor because the Russians shot him, and no medicine because the Germans took it all for their soldiers, so she died. Before the war, Dovydas had both arms, but it was blown off by the Germans. Before the war, Magdalena and Dovydas had a herd of beautiful fat dairy cows, but the Russians took them all away. Now they live a quiet life with some angry geese and a scared goat, and just three arms between two people.

Magdalena lays Mia on a rug by the fire and gently peels away her damp, filthy clothes. She gasps when she sees the tiny bundle of bones that our little sister's body has become.

She washes Mia's papery skin with a cloth soaked in warm, oily water. She clothes her in a soft white nightdress that must once have belonged to her own little daughter, then she cuts Mia's greasy matted hair off at the roots.

Magdalena wraps Mia in blankets and holds her to her chest. She sits in the rocking chair by the fire and sings Lithuanian lullabies. She spoons water between Mia's dry, cracked lips. She strokes Mia's feverish forehead and kisses her thin white cheeks and tells her she is precious. And she does it day after day after day.

While Magdalena takes care of Mia, Otto and I work with Dovydas, from early in the morning before the sun has even risen to late in the evening, long after the sun has sunk. We dig up potatoes from his fields, furrowing through snow and mud and icy water. We work to pay for the kindness that Magdalena and Dovydas have shown. To pay for the plenty they have given. More plenty than we have seen in almost a year.

We dig and scrape, and haul cart after cart of potatoes into the barn. We try to be Dovydas's second arm, to return what our fellow Germans have taken away.

We dig and scrape and haul, and all the while Dovydas looks over his shoulder and tells us, 'Watch! Beware!' because the Russians run Lithuania now and we mustn't let them see us.

'The Russians hate Germans,' he says. As if we don't already know it!

'*We* hate the Russians!' shouts Otto. He blushes, then mumbles, 'Except for the good ones.'

I know he is thinking about Dmitri and Alexi and Viktor. And maybe also Dog, because he has probably become a Russian calf by now. Poor little thing.

Dovydas nods. He understands that things are complicated.

Russian, German, Lithuanian—they can be both friends and enemies. But mostly enemies when there is a war . . . or a horrible mess *after* a war.

'Just make sure the Russians never catch you here,' he warns.

'What would they do to us?' asks Otto.

'To you?' Dovydas shrugs. 'It is not what they would do to *you*. It is what they would do to *us*, to Magdalena and me.'

'What would they do to you?' I whisper.

Dovydas wipes his hand across his brow. It's an awkward gesture, one he must have done with the other hand before the Germans blew it off.

'The Russians forbid us to help the Germans,' he says. 'Even the lonely little Germans who are running all over our country begging for food and shelter and love. Lithuanians who are kind to German children will be arrested and sent to Siberia to the work camps.'

Otto gasps. 'The work camps!' Bruno and Josef told us about such places. People are sent to the icy cold region of Siberia and worked like slaves. And they don't come back.

Dovydas plunges his spade into the earth and pulls up a clump of mud.

I rush forward to separate the potatoes from the mud and whisper, 'Don't worry, Dovydas. We won't let the Russians find us. We are wild children. We are good at hiding. We are good at running away. We are good at slipping through traps. We are wild like wolves, and we won't be caught.'

It can be both good and bad to have grown so wild.

Three days pass and Magdalena is still cradling Mia in her arms, rocking back and forth, hugging, kissing, singing Lithuanian lullabies.

Mia doesn't move. She doesn't make a sound except to wheeze and moan. Her skin has turned from white to gray. Gray skin is worse than blue lips.

More snow falls and the soil hardens. Otto and I work on and on in the field with Dovydas until our fingers are raw and our feet are frozen and we can no longer straighten our backs. We work like donkeys until we are crying with exhaustion.

Dovydas tells us to stop, *begs* us to stop, but we don't. We work to pay for the kindness he and Magdalena have shown us. And we work so that the mountain of potatoes in the barn grows big enough to hide behind if the Russians come. But mostly we work so that we do not have to think about Mia.

We would rather cry over raw fingers and aching backs that will heal one day than a precious sister who will slip away forever.

After five days, the harvest is done. Dovydas feeds us boiled potatoes and goat's milk and makes up our bed in front of the kitchen stove.

I glance across at Magdalena, where she is rocking Mia back and forth before the open fire. Magdalena is weeping!

Otto slips his hand into mine.

I whisper, barely a breath, 'Maybe she's crying for her own little girl.'

Otto squeezes my fingers, and I know he is thinking of the *other* maybe. The one that I won't say out loud. The one that will break our hearts and change us forever.

We stare and Magdalena weeps. Dovydas kneels at her side.

Otto squeezes my fingers so hard that it hurts.

I stop breathing. Tears run down my cheeks, and I wonder how I will ever face Mama again, even in my thoughts.

How will I ever face Otto again? I have lost Mia.

'Liesl!'

I look up. Dovydas has his hand on my shoulder and is telling me to come.

I shake my head. Dovydas insists.

Otto and I follow him to the fire, to the chair where Magdalena is weeping softly, no longer rocking, but pressing Mia into her chest.

Magdalena's weeps turn into sobs, and Otto begins to cry, and I join in.

Mia is gone. Gone!

I moan and fall to my knees and howl.

And then I stop, because a soft little voice cuts through the misery.

'Mia want Liesl.'

CHAPTER 40

How do you thank someone for saving your sister? You can hug them and kiss them and bathe them in your tears, which is what Otto and I do, but it doesn't seem enough.

You can shout, 'Thank you! Thank you! Thank you!' over and over again, which we do, but that also seems too little. Even when we learn the Lithuanian words and say it over and over again once more.

You can pay them with gold and silver and jewels, which I try. I rip open Mia's coat, take out all the jewelry that Mama sewed into the lining, and pour it into Magdalena's lap. 'No!' she cries, her face filled with horror, as though I have just dumped a cowpat on her apron.

'As payment,' I explain, 'for kindness and help.' I sob with gratitude. 'For love!'

Dovydas scoops Mama's jewels into his hand and gives them back. 'Love is free. It never needs payment.'

He shows us where we can hide the jewels, tucked beneath a floorboard in the larder. But we must part with other treasures.

Baby is rotten and a carrier of disease. Into the fire she goes. Mia stares in horror, but she is too weak to scream, too weak to cry, too weak to even shed a tear.

Likewise, the dirty, flea-filled blanket is burned—outside because it's too big and damp and smelly to stuff into the fireplace.

Next, Magdalena searches our clothes. She finds the two family photos and takes them to the kitchen stove.

'No!' I shout. The photos are the only way we can catch a glimpse of Mama and Papa, Oma, and Opa. Without them, Mia will not remember what they look like.

'If the Russians find the photos, they will see that you are German,' says Magdalena. 'The house, the clothes, the faces—they all prove who you really are.'

Into the flames the photos go.

Magdalena stares at us, hands on hips, mouth screwed up in thought. 'Your names are so very German too,' she says. 'It's good that you hide if the Russians come. But if they find you, you must pretend to be Lithuanian. It is your best chance. . . . It is *our* best chance.'

I think of the icy wastelands of Siberia and shudder.

'From now on,' says Magdalena, in her schoolteacher

voice, 'you, Otto, will be called Ignas, and you, Liesl, will be known as Lukrecija. Ignas and Lukrecija are good Lithuanian names.'

'Ignas?' Otto wrinkles his nose, then shrugs. 'All right.'

'Lukrecija,' I murmur. I force a smile onto my lips and nod at Magdalena, but a little pain stabs in my chest.

Magdalena walks over to the crib by the fire where Mia is now fast asleep. She strokes Mia's cheek, and her face is filled with love as she whispers, 'And Mia will be called Svajone.'

'Svajone,' I echo.

Magdalena lifts Mia into her arms and rocks her from side to side. 'Svajone,' she coos. 'It means "dream."'

I do not like the idea of Mia being called a dream. It sounds like something that is too light, too unreal. Mia is still pale and listless. She sleeps nearly all the time. She is so weak and tired that she doesn't even snore. Snoring would take too much energy. If Mia is a dream, she might always be floating around, thin and pale, just a whisper of her old self. Or she might simply fade away to nothing. I want her to be named after something firm and full, like a fish or a rock or a plum. 'Plum' is a good solid name.

Magdalena inspects our coats. They are dirty and have holes in the elbows and buttons missing, but they are the only heavy winter clothes we have. She picks off the labels from inside the collars because they are German and throws them into the stove. Then she cleans and patches and sews on wooden buttons until our coats are almost as good as new.

'Lithuanian coats!' she declares, and holds them up for us to see.

German coats pretending to be Lithuanian, I think. But I don't say it out loud. Magdalena is only doing what she must to keep us all safe.

Last of all, Magdalena takes away our words. 'From now on,' she says, 'you speak Lithuanian.'

Otto's eyes grow wide. 'But we don't know *how* to speak Lithuanian.'

'I will teach you,' she says. 'First of all, you must say, "*Mano vardas* Ignas." It means "My name is Ignas."'

Otto copies: 'Mano vardas Ignas.'

Magdalena clasps her hands to her cheeks and smiles.

Otto bows.

'Now your turn, Lukrecija,' says Magdalena, turning to me.

Again, a pain stabs in my chest, but I say, 'Mano vardas Lukrecija.'

And so we begin to vanish.

That night, as Otto and I lie in our bed by the kitchen stove, I run through the Wolf family tree just as Opa taught me. I say Opa's and Oma's full names—first, middle, and last— and the full names of all their children and their husbands and wives, and every other family member we have met. Even Uncle Fritz, who smells of bacon and hates children.

'What are you doing?' moans Otto. 'You're keeping me awake.'

'I'm remembering,' I explain. 'I'm remembering who we are.'

'We need to forget,' he says. 'Mano vardas Ignas, remember?'

'No, Otto!' I snap. 'We must never forget. We are Wolfs and we will always be Wolfs. We can *pretend* that we are someone else, but in our hearts we must always be Otto Friedrich Wolf, Liesl Anna Wolf, and Mia Hilda Wolf. Because one day, we will find the other Wolfs who we belong to, and we will live happily ever after.'

Otto is silent for a long time. Then, finally, he whispers, 'But I don't mind being a Lithuanian boy called Ignas. I like Magdalena and Dovydas. And I like it here. Besides, I don't believe in happily-ever-afters anymore. I think there is just happily *enough* . . . if we are lucky. We shouldn't expect too much, Lukrecija.'

And the pain that has been poking at my heart all day stabs so hard and so deep that I begin to cry.

CHAPTER 41

It is Christmas Eve. Twelve months since Papa went missing in action.

And then so much more went missing. Mama, Oma, and Opa. Otto's eighth birthday. My twelfth birthday. East Prussia. Our homeland, East Prussia, is no longer there. Poland owns the south. Russia controls the north. Everything old and beautiful and German is being wiped away.

But now it is Christmas Eve and we must think only of good things. We have a new mama and a new papa, and our precious little Mia is strong enough to sit and walk and talk. The few words she murmurs are Lithuanian, and there is no joy in them, no accompanying laughter or clapping. But I try not to mind. Mia is alive and growing stronger and stronger, and that is all that matters for now.

Otto and I begin the day by helping in the barn. I milk

Roze the goat. She is white and smelly, but I like her and she seems to like me.

I thought Mia might like Roze too. She loved Dog and Yummy Cow so very much. But she's not interested in Roze. Perhaps she has no energy to love anyone or anything new. Or maybe she is still thinking about losing Yummy Cow and doesn't want to give her heart so freely again.

I sing to Roze while I milk—quiet little German songs that Dovydas can't hear. Roze blinks and bends her neck around so she can nibble the hem of my skirt. She nibbles in time to my singing, and I like to think that she is a Lithuanian goat with a German heart.

Otto collects the eggs, changes the water in the troughs, and scatters grain for the geese. The geese are cranky. They chase Otto around and around the barn—one great white gaggle, honking, pecking, hissing, even when he offers them the whole bucket of grain.

'Stop biting!' shouts Otto at last. He says it in German. He still breaks into German when he's cross or scared. 'Stop biting or I'll kick you in the pants!'

The geese stop. One flaps its wings. Then, together, they turn and bustle away.

Dovydas leans on his pitchfork and laughs. 'Brave boy, Ignas! I am proud of you! But I'm not sure that geese wear pants. And next time, you must say it in Lithuanian.'

Dovydas spends the next five minutes teaching Otto how to scold the geese in our new language. Otto mimics both

Dovydas's words and facial expressions, blushing all the time. He is so hungry for a papa's love.

After breakfast, Otto and Dovydas trudge through the snow into the forest, where they cut spruce branches to decorate the house. They return, red-cheeked and laughing, laden down with greenery. They decorate the fireplace and the doorways, and the scent of pine fills the house.

'I wish we had a proper tree,' says Otto, 'with candles at the ends of all the branches.'

Dovydas ruffles Otto's hair—hair that is clean and blond once more—and says, 'A tree would be nice, Ignas. But trees are what *German* families have at Christmastime. Lithuanians like us have spruce branches.'

It's a pretty tradition, but not as pretty as a fine Christmas tree with real candles flickering at the tips of its branches. There's nothing like a German Christmas tree.

Magdalena and I clean the house from one end to the other, then spend the rest of the day making a Christmas feast. There are twelve courses, one to represent each of Jesus's apostles.

My mouth waters as Magdalena describes the treats— herring, salads, Christmas cookies, poppy-seed milk, cranberry drink, wafers, baked potatoes, fruits, chocolate. But when we walk into the larder, all we can find are potatoes, goat's cheese, onions, today's goose eggs, and flour.

Magdalena waves her arm as though she is revealing a

treasure trove of delicacies, then bursts out laughing. 'So,' she says, 'we might not have so many of the right ingredients, but we are clever and we will do our best.'

When we sit down at the Christmas table that night, we are all newly bathed, our hair shining, our cheeks red and smooth from scrubbing.

There are twelve courses laid out along the table, although there is a lot of potato about them. We have boiled potatoes, mashed potatoes, roast potatoes, two kinds of potato dumplings, and potatoes cut into three different shapes—cubes, stars, and straws. The other four courses are boiled eggs, fried onion, goat's cheese, and a cranberry drink, which Magdalena calls *kisielius*.

'Marvelous!' cries Dovydas. He jumps up from his seat and kisses Magdalena on the cheek, then he kisses Mia and me on the tops of our heads. 'My clever girls!'

We eat and laugh and sing Lithuanian Christmas hymns. Then halfway through dinner, Dovydas disappears and returns wearing a scruffy white beard made from goat's hair and carrying a cloth sack.

'Look!' cries Magdalena. 'Saint Nicholas is here!'

Otto jumps up from the table and runs at Dovydas. He wraps his arms around him and shouts, 'Thank you! Thank you! I love you, Papa! I love you, Papa!'

Dovydas laughs and says, 'But I am Saint Nicholas, and you don't even know yet what gifts I bring!'

The gifts are beautiful. For Mia, a little rag doll that

Magdalena has stitched late at night. The doll has yellow hair and blue eyes.

'Just like our precious little Svajone,' says Magdalena.

Mia takes the doll and stares at it. She turns it upside down and back the right way. She looks at me and I smile and nod. And, at last, Mia smiles. It is soft and shy, but it lights up the room like a thousand Christmas candles blazing from a German Christmas tree. It is a miracle. A treasure.

'She's a very pretty dolly,' I say. 'What will you call her?'

Mia blinks but does not answer. She always loved naming dolls and toys and animals. But not now.

'Ona,' sings Magdalena, naming the new doll.

'Ona,' says Mia. She hugs the doll to her chest. It is the first sign of affection she has shown since she was ill.

Magdalena and Dovydas look at each other, and I see sadness and love and something else that might be hope.

For Otto, there is a toy horse and wagon that Dovydas has made from wood. The wagon is filled with real seeds.

'Rye,' explains Dovydas. 'So you can help me with the sowing when spring comes.'

Otto beams with pride.

For me, there is an apron and a scarf, white with red embroidery, like Magdalena's own. She wraps the apron around my waist and covers my hair with the scarf.

'Now,' she says, stepping back and smiling, 'you look like a proper Lithuanian girl!'

We return to the table and eat until our bellies are bursting.

We talk and sing and thank God for his blessings of food and shelter and this strange new world that we call Peace.

And it feels as if we are a family.

A Lithuanian family—Magdalena, Dovydas, Ignas, Svajone, Ona, and Lukrecija.

A happy family.

So why do I feel the same panic that I felt in my white dream?

And what is that horrible pain in my chest?

The winter is long and harsh. The snow keeps on coming and never melts away. But we are warm and dry thanks to Magdalena and Dovydas. We would never have survived without them.

Mia's hair grows back, the stubble becoming soft golden curls, and her cheeks grow round and plump once more. She drinks sweet warm goat's milk and eats potato dumplings, bread, soup, soft-boiled goose eggs. But she never rubs food into her hair. Not once. This makes me unbearably sad.

Mia speaks in whispers and sings in a breathy, high-pitched voice. All her words and tunes are Lithuanian, and I wonder if she remembers any German. Does she know that we were once German children? Does she miss Mama and Papa? Can she even picture them?

Mia plays with Ona, her new doll, but at nighttime she leaves her tossed aside on the floor. I cuddle Mia, trying to remind her that this is how we show love. But she never cuddles back. Not for me. Not for Magdalena. Not even for Otto.

In the evenings, we sit by the fire and Dovydas tells us folktales. They are Lithuanian folktales filled with bears, hedgehogs, ravens, kings, and witches. So many witches.

The witches slink out of the stories and into my dreams. My dreams turn into nightmares. I try to think of the innocent hedgehogs as I fall asleep at night, but the witches still work their wicked way into my dreams—ragged, gaunt, and hungry, watching and waiting for a lone child to wander their way. Sometimes a witch is lucky. She seizes a child, and the child is always Mia.

I wake, sweaty and breathless, and tell myself it's just a dream. But the witches keep coming back, and they force their way into my daytime thoughts as well as my nighttime dreams.

The first time I see her, I am gazing across the snowy meadows to the forest, and there she is in the distance—a dark, ragged figure standing between the trees. Watching. Waiting. I can barely see her, but I know what she is. A witch!

I stare until she slinks away, disappearing deep into the forest.

'She's gone,' I whisper, trying to feel relieved, but I can't. The witch returns. Two weeks later, then one. Again and again. She looks so real, even as she blends into the darkness between the trees. But every time I drag Magdalena to the window to point her out, she is gone.

I know the witch is a figment of my imagination. I know that I am sad and muddled by the way Mia has changed, as though she has been snatched away from Otto and me. I know that the witch lurking in the forest is just another form of the pain that is lurking in my chest.

But still, I keep watch over Mia, night and day, making sure that she never wanders outside into the snow alone.

Magdalena gives us school lessons that help fill the long, dark days. Now that we are fed and warm and safe, Otto learns quickly. And with Dovydas watching, he tries harder and harder, eager to please his new papa and keen to show that he is smart enough to become a vet one day.

But the reading and writing is Lithuanian, not German, and every success takes us further and further away from our old life.

Every day, I see the Wolf children vanishing a little bit more.

First Mia. Now Otto.

The pain in my chest stabs harder and deeper than I ever thought possible. And I spot the gaunt, ragged witch slinking about between the trees at the edge of the forest more and more.

CHAPTER 42

It's springtime and the snow is melting. Dovydas, Otto, and I are returning from the early morning chores in the barn when the Russians arrive. Four of them. On a truck. Big and dirty, with guns slung over their shoulders. They are looking for pigs. The Red Army is on the move again, and the soldiers are hungry.

'There are no pigs,' says Dovydas in Russian. 'We once had many cows, but your army took them all away.'

One of the soldiers is staring at Otto and me. Can he see that we are German?

I tell my legs not to wobble, my cheeks not to burn. I tighten my scarf beneath my chin and look down at my apron to reassure myself that I look like a normal Lithuanian girl.

Otto waves and says, *Labas rytas.* But I can see the twitching of his fingers and the fear in his eyes.

Dovydas chuckles and pulls Otto to himself. 'My son,' he explains, again in Russian. 'He has just said good morning in Lithuanian.'

One of the soldiers goes into the house and returns with Magdalena and Mia.

Mia is clinging to Magdalena's body like a baby monkey and hides her face in Magdalena's shoulder. I know that Mia won't talk, and if she does, all her words will be perfect Lithuanian. It is, after all, the only language she speaks nowadays.

'Pigs!' shouts the soldier who seems to be in charge.

I hope he's talking about the animals, not us.

He points his gun toward the barn, and we all go inside.

Dovydas catches my eye and smiles. I know he is trying to say, 'It's all right, Lukrecija. Keep calm and everything will be all right.'

Roze the goat is frightened by the four strange men. Or maybe she senses our fear and knows that something is wrong. She bleats and scrambles to the top of the potato mountain. Potatoes tumble and topple and roll all over the barn.

Otto steps on one. His foot flies from under him, and he falls flat on his back. The geese, seeing a marvelous opportunity, rush forward, flapping, hissing, and honking. They peck his hands and his knees and his tummy and his face.

'Stop biting!' cries Otto, swinging his arms and kicking his feet. 'Stop biting! You horrible, nasty, stupid, ugly geese! Stop biting or I will kick you in the pants!'

It doesn't matter that we have tossed aside our German names and burned our family photos and the German labels from the insides of our coats. It doesn't matter that we sing Lithuanian songs and believe in Lithuanian witches, or that we have been doing Lithuanian school lessons for three months and speak nothing but Lithuanian with Dovydas and Magdalena. It doesn't matter that Magdalena and Dovydas have cared for us as their own children. None of it matters. Because, in his anger and fright, my brother has forgotten to be a Lithuanian boy called Ignas Balkas and has become himself once more. He is Otto Friedrich Wolf, a boy who loses his temper and shouts at geese. And he does it in perfect German.

Otto has given us away!

One of the Russian soldiers rushes forward and pulls Otto out from the gaggle of geese. I hold my breath, waiting for the soldier to strike Otto across the face.

Otto will be struck, and Mia will be tossed aside like a piece of rubbish, and I will be kicked. Then Magdalena and Dovydas will be dragged out of the barn and thrown onto the back of the truck and sent to Siberia for hiding dirty German children. And we will be abandoned and alone, living wild in the forest like wolves once more.

I hold my breath and wait for the barn and the rest of the world to collapse in on me.

But the soldier does not hit Otto. He plants him on his feet and brushes straw from his coat. He ruffles Otto's blond hair, smiles, and says in Russian, 'I hate geese too. They are evil.'

Otto's eyes are as wide as dinner plates. 'Thank you,' says Dovydas, also in Russian.

The soldiers take a quick look around the barn. They laugh at Roze perched atop the potatoes, bleating at the rafters. They kick at the geese and send them scattering. They nod to Magdalena and to Dovydas. Then they leave.

Otto and I run to each other and hug.

Magdalena joins us with Mia, and she and Dovydas wrap their three arms around us.

Magdalena weeps. But Dovydas laughs.

'We are the luckiest family in Lithuania,' he cries. 'The soldiers who came to our farm today speak nothing but Russian. They *understand* nothing but Russian. Lithuanian, German, French, English—it all sounds the same to them.'

'So when I spoke German, they didn't realize?' asks Otto.

Dovydas chuckles. 'No. They just heard a scared little Lithuanian boy yelping and crying out for help.'

'And they gave it,' I said.

Russian kindness for a German boy in a Lithuanian barn. Nothing makes sense anymore.

It is late at night, and I am still tossing and turning when Otto whispers, 'Liesl, are you awake?'

It's the first time he has called me Liesl in a long time. 'Yes, Otto,' I reply, a soft, warm feeling in my heart.

'I liked speaking German out in the open today,' he says.

'Even when I realized what I was doing and that it was really, *really* dangerous. The words felt so good.'

'Yes,' I reply. 'They sounded good too.'

We are both silent, and I know we are both thinking about what could have happened.

'German words feel right in my mouth,' he says.

'Yes,' I agree.

'And in my head.'

'Yes.'

'And in my heart.'

I wrap my arm around him. 'Yes!'

Otto sniffs and wipes his sleeve across his face. We are silent for a long time, and I know that he is waiting for the words I will say next.

'But from now on,' I whisper at last, 'you and I must speak Lithuanian. Always. Even with Roze and the geese. Even with each other in the middle of the night. Even in our heads and in our hearts. It is the only way we will become fully Ignas and fully Lukrecija. And that is the only way we will ever be truly safe—you, me, Mia, Magdalena, Dovydas.'

Otto sniffs.

I shake him and say, 'Otto! Do you hear me?'

'Yes,' he whimpers, then adds, 'but can we sing just one last German song?'

I squeeze his shoulder. 'I think that's a lovely idea.'

I start singing the duckling song, because I don't get to sing it with Mia anymore. Mia has already become a

Lithuanian girl called Svajone who only sings Lithuanian nursery rhymes.

I sing about the ducklings on the lake and Otto joins in. We sing about the doves on the roof, then the chickens in the straw, and the goslings in the pond. It is all so very simple, but so very beautiful. German words about German birds filling our German hearts.

We sing it over and over again. Over and over.

Until Otto's words become slurred and, finally, he falls asleep.

Otto sleeps, but I keep singing. I don't want to sleep because I know that when I wake, the German words must all be gone. Liesl Anna Wolf, the German girl, must be gone.

I lie awake, singing my way through every German song I can remember. My eyes start to droop, but I am not ready to vanish, so I slip into my coat and boots and creep outside. The cold night air slaps me awake. I pull my coat more tightly around me and I walk. Across the fields and into the forest. And as I walk, I talk out loud, reciting German poems, telling German fairy tales. I don't want to stop, because when the songs and rhymes and stories and all the German words are gone, I will be gone. Liesl Anna Wolf will be no more.

I walk and talk and sing until my feet drag and my words fade to sobs. I stop in the middle of the forest and stare at my hands. I am about to vanish, and the pain in my chest is so sharp and deep that I think I will die.

I have done many wicked things since we fled from our

home in East Prussia. I have stolen and pillaged and cursed and killed animals with my bare hands and told lie after lie after lie. But this thing that I am about to do, this vanishing, feels like the most dreadful yet.

For when I vanish, all the Wolf children will have vanished—Liesl Anna Wolf, Otto Friedrich Wolf, and Mia Hilda Wolf. And once we are gone, Mama will never be able to find us again.

There will be no happily-ever-after. It was all a lie from the very start.

I squeeze my hands into fists and scream between the trees, my final German words. 'I hate Hitler!'

CHAPTER 43

My words have long turned to frost.

I am surrounded by silence.

The Wolfs have vanished. Me. Otto. Mia. Mama. Papa.
Opa. Oma. Gone.

Behind me, a twig snaps. 'Who's there?' I hiss.

Nobody answers.

'Otto?' I whisper.

But Otto doesn't reply.

There is another snap, closer this time.

I spin around and stare, openmouthed, terrified, as a
body shifts from the darkness into a beam of moonlight. It
is a woman, gaunt, dressed from head to toe in rags. Her
head is wrapped in a shawl so that all I can see is her nose
and eyes.

It is the witch I have seen from the window. She is no

longer lurking in my imagination. She is no longer slinking about in the distance. She is here and she is real!

I step back and whimper, 'Please. Please don't hurt me.'

The witch holds up both hands, palms toward me. Her nails are jagged and filthy.

'If you let me go,' I say, 'I won't tell anyone you are here.'

'Liesl,' says the witch.

My neck prickles. She knows my name! She's been watching, waiting for me to come into the forest alone.

'Liesl.'

All this time I've been worried about Mia, but it's *me* who is about to be snatched away.

'Liesl,' she says again, but this time there is a softness to the words.

A strange happiness floods through me.

'Liesl,' she sings, her voice floating around me in a soothing warm wave.

This is real Lithuanian magic. The witch is casting a spell over me so I can't run away. I press my hands to my chest and close my eyes.

'Liesl.' The voice is so very lovely. 'Open your eyes.'

I don't want to open my eyes. I don't want this warmth and happiness to end. Even if it means I am taken deeper and deeper into the forest and can never return. I have already vanished, so what does it matter anyway?

'Open your eyes,' pleads the voice once more. Slowly, reluctantly, I open my eyes.

The witch pulls back her shawl and smiles at me. 'Liesl,' she sighs.

I shriek and run at the witch. I run so hard that I knock her from her feet and send her sprawling onto the forest floor. I throw myself onto her and wrap my arms around her and scream and howl like a wild wolf.

I scream and howl and cry, 'Mama! Mama! Mama!'

CHAPTER 44

Everyone deserves a happily-ever-after.

Even German children. Even wild children.

My mama is here. My real mama, Anna Edith Wolf. 'Mama! Mama! Mama!' I sob over and over again, until my voice runs dry and my tears also.

Mama and I hug, and then we touch each other's face. Cheeks and nose and eyelids. We stare at each other, then hug again, unable to keep apart. Because it's been so long. Because it feels so good. But also, because I'm scared.

If I let go, Mama might vanish once more. Into the dark forest. Into my imagination. I cannot lose her again. I have lost too much already.

Even now I am aching, because there is so much sadness squeezed in with the joy. Mama is here. But Papa is not. My kind, gentle papa who smelled of soap and schnapps and nutmeg is gone. Forever.

Oma and Opa too.

Our home. Our school. Our entire village.

And there are those we found and loved along the way. Dmitri. Alexi. Viktor. Karl. Bruno and Josef. Mozart, Dog, and Yummy Cow. They might still be ours to love if we had met them at another time. But we didn't, and we have lost them, too.

But Mama is here.

'Mama.' I press harder, closer. 'You really are here.'

'I found you!' Mama laughs and cries. 'I found you!'

'But *how*?' I ask. 'After all this time.'

'I never stopped looking, Liesl. I never gave up. I searched in every town and village around the Vistula Lagoon. I knocked on doors. I stared through windows. I looked in barns. I walked through forests and fields, calling out your names. For days . . . weeks . . . months.'

'You might have passed nearby,' I say. 'If only you'd gone a little farther to the left or right . . . If only you'd shouted our names one more time . . . If only . . .' I stop.

You can break your heart wondering such things.

We walk slowly through the forest, back toward the farm, and Mama continues her story.

'The war ended, and maybe I *would* have found you, but the Russians caught me and forced me to work for them. Me and lots of other German women.'

'In Siberia?' I gasp.

Mama shakes her head sadly. 'There was plenty of work in our own beautiful country, cleaning up the mess the Russians had made just months before. We shoveled rubble, stacked bricks, dug holes and buried dead horses, made bonfires and burned broken wagons and wardrobes and strollers . . . But I never stopped thinking of you, praying for you, my darling children. I promised myself that the day I was free I would start looking for you once more.'

'And you did!' I cry. 'You did keep looking!'

'Yes, Liesl. I did.' She squeezes me tighter. 'When the Russians let me go months later, I was starving. *Everyone* in East Prussia was starving. So I traveled back and forth to Lithuania for food—but every time I returned to East Prussia, I looked for you once more.'

'But we were *here*, Mama,' I say, clinging to her. 'You were here, and we were here, and you were looking in the wrong spot! If only . . .' I stop myself once more.

Mama nods. 'But on my last trip, I met a strange little girl—dirty, skinny, all alone. I offered her my protection, my love, but she said she didn't need my help. She would soon find her boyfriend, Karl, and he would take care of her.'

I gasp at Karl's name. 'Charlotte?'

'Yes.' Mama sighs. 'Charlotte. She saw the family photo I carried and said she knew you. I thought she was lying, but she pointed to each one of you and called you by name. And that's when she told me that you too had traveled to Lithuania.'

Of course Charlotte said nothing about knocking me off the train. But I can't be cross. Because in the end, whether she meant to or not, Charlotte helped.

'So I stayed in Lithuania,' says Mama. 'I wandered from village to village, farm to farm. Watching. Waiting. Hoping. I came back to this farm many times. I saw no children, but I had a feeling . . . I cannot explain.' Mama's steps slow. 'Then a week ago, I saw a boy walking from the house to the barn.'

'Otto,' I whisper.

'There was something familiar about him, even from so far away. But he didn't swagger the way my Otto swaggers.' Mama pauses. 'Then a man I thought must be his papa shouted across the yard, calling him Ignas. And the boy's words were not German.' She lowers her voice. 'Even so, I couldn't shake that feeling. I kept returning to the edge of the forest . . . to watch . . . to wait . . . but barely *daring* to hope. For I saw no girls. No Liesl. No Mia.'

Mama stares at me, a question about Mia hanging silently in the air. But she doesn't ask. And I do not tell. Because how can I explain what has happened to my beautiful baby sister? Instead, I babble, 'The papa is Dovydas and there is a mama, Magdalena, and we changed our names so the Russians would think we were Lithuanian, not German, but it doesn't matter that you didn't know, because the feeling you had was right, wasn't it, Mama? It was real, because we *are* here. And you waited and believed and now, tonight, you found me!'

We reach the house and Mama stops. She stares at the

door, her hands pressed against her chest, her eyes full of joy and fear.

'Otto is in there?' she whispers. 'My naughty little Otto?' I open the door, take Mama by the hand, and lead her inside to where my brother is snuggled up in bed. He is a mess of blond hair and pajamas and blankets. 'Otto,' I whisper, shaking him by the shoulder.

He looks up through puffy eyes. He yelps and, in a flash, he is out of bed and wrapped in Mama's arms.

'Mama!' he cries. 'Mama! Is it a dream? Or are you really here?'

Mama smothers his nose and cheeks and forehead and eyes with kisses. 'I'm here,' she whispers. 'I'm here. I'm here. I'm here.'

Magdalena appears at the bedroom door, Svajone on her hip. Dovydas stands behind them.

Mama looks up. Her hands drop to her sides and she whimpers. She stares at me. 'Mia? Mia is here?'

The little girl who *looks* like our sister is here. Her cheeks are plump. Her golden hair is springy with curls. She speaks and walks and sings. But she is not Mia. Mia is gone. The German words. The laughter. The snoring. The shine in her eyes. The cuddles and love. All of Mia is gone. This is Svajone.

Gently, Magdalena lets Svajone slip from her hip to the floor. She keeps her hands cupped around Svajone's tiny shoulders and, for a moment, I think she will refuse to let her go.

But then, softly, slowly, Magdalena kisses the little girl's golden head and steps back to lean against Dovydas.

We all watch in silence.

Svajone blinks. She rubs her sleepy eyes. She walks toward us.

Mama drops to her knees and holds out her arms. Svajone stops and takes one step back.

'Mia, baby girl,' coos Mama. 'I'm so very happy I have found you.'

A smile twitches around the corners of Svajone's mouth. The smile takes hold and stretches wide, lighting up her face, and the room, and our hearts, like a million candles on a thousand German Christmas trees.

Svajone walks forward. As Mama's arms close around her, she reaches up with her little-girl arms and returns the hug, rubbing her cheek against Mama's chest, huddling in as close as she can go, turning into Mia.

Otto takes my hand, and together we step forward and wrap our arms around our mama and our sister and each other, and we become a Mama-Mia-Otto-Liesl blob. We hug and squeeze, closer, tighter, until a voice squeals in German, 'Ouch! Ouch! Too much love! Too much love!'

But there is no such thing as too much love!

Love keeps a brother and two sisters together, no matter how much the world tries to tear them apart.

Love keeps a mama looking for her children, even when it seems hopeless that she will ever find them again.

Love reaches deep down into the heart of a little girl who has lost herself in sorrow and welcomes her back home. One hug squeezes Svajone away and brings Mia, our beautiful, precious little Mia, bursting to life once more.

Love draws Magdalena and Dovydas into our blob, cuddling, pressing, laughing, forming a new family.

There is no such thing as too much love, so we keep hugging, and Mia's squeals turn to giggles, and we find, at last, our happily-ever-after.

ACKNOWLEDGMENTS

I am truly blessed to have a writing life full of clever and supportive people.

Writing *We Are Wolves* has been a joy and a challenge. There is always a joy in discovering, writing, and sharing new stories. The challenge came in finding the balance between creating an interesting and appropriate story for young readers while being respectful of the real Wolfskinder and the horrors they endured. Thank you to my fellow writers and dear friends, Amy Doak and Lorraine Marwood, and my son, Klaus Nannestad, who listened and affirmed and provided wonderful advice. I hope you all know how much your support meant to me at this time—and always means to me.

Eddie (Kate Burnitt), my in-house editor, and Chris Kunz, were the first people to be excited by my story idea.

Thank you for encouraging me to write this book. Eddie, you continue to be the voice in my head as I write. Your years of skillful editing and nurturing have helped shape my writing.

I have had brilliant people at HarperCollins Books in Australia working with me on the manuscript—Chren Byng, my publisher; Nicola O'Shea, my copy editor; and Eve Tonelli, my in-house editor. And Jane Novak, my literary agent, is always there, cheering me on. Thanks to all of you.

It has been a delight to see my story come alive in Martina Heiduczek's beautiful and sensitive illustrations. Each picture melts my heart. Thank you, Martina. I am in awe of your artistic talent.

I have been overwhelmed by the enormous amount of support from my fellow writers. Thank you to all who made the time to read this book and have been so very generous with their words.

Most of all, I am grateful to my husband, Carsten. You have mastered the art of listening to my doubts, obsessions, and wonderings, then replying with the words, 'But that's all part of your writing process. That's how it is with every book, remember? This one will be brilliant.' You also know when I need coffee and hugs. Thank you!